PETER
THE DA

REGINALD Evelyn Peter Southouse Cheyney (1896-1951) was born in Whitechapel in the East End of London. After serving as a lieutenant during the First World War, he worked as a police reporter and freelance investigator until he found success with his first Lemmy Caution novel. In his lifetime Cheyney was a prolific and wildly successful author, selling, in 1946 alone, over 1.5 million copies of his books. His work was also enormously popular in France, and inspired Jean-Luc Godard's character of the same name in his dystopian sci-fi film *Alphaville*. The master of British noir, in Lemmy Caution Peter Cheyney created the blueprint for the tough-talking, hard-drinking pulp fiction detective.

PETER CHEYNEY

THE DARK STREET

DEAN STREET PRESS

Published by Dean Street Press 2022

All Rights Reserved

First published in 1944

Cover by DSP

ISBN 978 1 915014 25 2

www.deanstreetpress.co.uk

To

MY WIFE
COMPANION IN ADVENTURE

"There are no shadows
in a dark street . . ."

CHAPTER ONE
The Things I Do For England

I

THE yellow mist seeped into the Place des Roses; bringing an almost evil quality to the *cul-de-sac*; rising only a few feet from the ground; creating the impression that there were no foundations to the small, dirty, dilapidated houses.

At the end of the *cul-de-sac* a thin knife-edge of light showed under the door of the wine shop. Inside the shop, which was dimly lit by an oil lamp, Fours leant over the counter at the end; regarded the board floor. About the place was the acrid smell of wine intermingled with the indescribable odour that came from his Mexican cigar—one of those things consisting of some indifferent leaves of tobacco rolled round a straw spinal column. From time to time he spat over the counter with precision into a tin can set in the middle of the floor.

Fours was big, fat, greasy, vaguely evil. His baggy brown velveteen trousers were tied up with a piece of string. His shirt, once of middle blue colour, was now dark blue with dirt. Through the open neck one could see his swarthy hair-covered chest.

His face was big and jowled. His skin glistened. His black moustache, the fierce eyebrows, set above little penetrating black eyes, the angle at which he wore a greasy black beret, conspired to give him the appearance of some decadent pirate who by some means had become transplanted into this wine shop in Paris in December, 1943.

Fours came round the counter. He took a tin jug from a hook on the wall opposite, held it under the spigot of a cask of wine, turned the spigot. When the jug was half filled, he put it to his mouth and drank. The wine tasted acid and bitter.

He hung up the jug, wiped his mouth with the back of his hand. He began to swear softly to himself, using indescribable oaths, an amazing conglomeration of words, seeking relief in the depths of obscenity.

One could swear. By God—that was all one could do! Whatever one did one was watched. Always there were people watching. Nobody could be trusted. And why not? Curse it, what else could you expect, when you could buy a man for a dozen square meals, or a pretty woman for a frock and a packet of sweets.

A hell of a place. Fours thought that Paris was a hell of a place. You couldn't get out, unless you got on the right side of those swine. And if you stayed, you starved on your feet or you were carted off by those black S.S. bastards to some other hell.

All you could do was to try and get your own back when you had a chance . . . *when* you had a chance . . .

Fours re-lit the Mexican cigar. It was damp through much chewing; tasted like brown paper.

He leaned up against the counter and waited. Outside he could smell the fog, creeping about the place like an infection, creeping about the place like every one crept in these days.

He spat. Under his breath he began to sing softly. He remembered the marching columns of other years. Under his breath he began to sing *Madelon*.

Duborg and Michaelson came up the Boulevard Clichy. They walked slowly, their hands in their pockets. Duborg was broad-shouldered, fat. He was a Gascon of good family. In his own particular way he was handsome. Women liked him.

Michaelson, the Englishman, was tall, thin, inclined to be weedy. Looking at Michaelson you would think he was without courage, either moral or physical. You would think he was a weakling. You would be wrong.

Duborg said: "My friend, I do not like it—not one little bit. I think it must have been that woman. The more I think of it the more certain I am that it was that woman. I hope her soul will be condemned to everlasting Hell!" Quietly, almost ruminatively, Duborg began to express a long series of blasphemous wishes about the woman.

Michaelson said quietly: "Does it matter? There is a chance that it may still be all right, you know."

Duborg said: "Yes. But something tells me that it will not be all right. I have the feeling," he went on, "that I have for a long time walked along a very straight and uninteresting road. I have hoped that the end of the road might be amusing. Now I think that the end of the road will not be so good."

Michaelson grinned. He said: "You've got indigestion, Henri. There's a fog coming up. That *might* be useful."

Duborg shrugged his shoulders. They turned into the Place des Roses. They walked quickly along the pavement into Fours' wine shop.

Duborg said: "*'Soir!* This place stinks."

Fours said: "Everything stinks. Paris stinks. I stink . . ." and, as an afterthought . . . "you also stink."

He took the metal jug off the hook, held it under the spigot of the wine cask until it was full; handed it to Duborg. Duborg drank half the wine. He drank it slowly.

He put the jug down on the counter. He said: "Well, Fours, has she been here?"

The other shook his head. "No," he said. "I regret, *mes amis*, she has not."

Duborg looked at Michaelson. He said: "It doesn't look so good!"

Michaelson said nothing. He turned his head a little as the door behind him opened. A small, rat-faced, boy, whose filthy and tattered clothes had barely enough strength to hang together, came into the shop.

Duborg's eyes brightened. He said: "Hey, Carlos, perhaps you know something?"

The boy said: "I know a lot. This afternoon they arrested Cerisette."

Duborg said quickly: "Who did?"

"The Vichy police," said Carlos. He spat graphically on to the floor. "Later they handed her over to those—So now you know."

Michaelson looked at Duborg—from Duborg to Fours. He smiled sadly. He said: "This is it."

Duborg said: "We get out of here. We must be quick. Otherwise they'll be on to Fours. If they've got her we're next on the list."

Michaelson said quietly: "You're perfectly right. So long, Fours. So long, Carlos."

The boy said in a quick, excited, voice: "I'm in on this."

Duborg looked at him and grinned. He called him a rude name. He said: "Listen, infant, we go now to—you know where. Follow quietly behind—twenty-five to thirty paces. It is foggy and very dark. Keep in the shadows. If we're wrong it doesn't matter. If we're right so much the better for you."

The boy opened his mouth to say something.

Duborg said in an affectionate tone: "Shut up, *canaille*. Do what you're told. Au 'voir, Fours." He went out of the shop.

Michaelson raised his hand to Fours; turned and followed him. He closed the door very quietly behind him.

The boy stood near the counter looking at Fours. His face was drawn—pathetic. The expression on Fours' face did not change. He endeavoured to spit, but found that his mouth was a little too dry for the process.

Duborg and Michaelson came out of the Place des Roses. They began to walk up the hill. The street was quiet and deserted. There was no sound. The fog, becoming thicker, blanketed everything that could be seen, turning concrete objects into nebulous shapes. A hundred yards up the hill they turned into a narrow alleyway. Now the boy Carlos was behind them—about thirty yards behind them—walking against the side of the houses, his eyes staring out of a white face straight in front of him. When he got to the corner of the turning, he waited.

On the other side, fifteen yards down the little street, Duborg was opening the door of a ramshackle house. Inside, he switched on a small electric torch; began to walk up the wooden stairs. Michaelson was close behind him.

The flight of stairs was narrow and curving. As they came round the curve Duborg stopped. He put one hand behind him; found Michaelson's shoulder. He squeezed it. Facing them, on the first landing, was a door. Beneath the door a gleam of light showed. Duborg sighed. They ascended the few remaining stairs, crossed the landing. Duborg threw open the door.

There were three men in the room. One of them was holding in his hand a Mauser automatic pistol. He was a short man, dressed in a cheap ready-made French suit. The hand holding the pistol hung limply by his side. His eyes were restless.

Duborg and Michaelson came into the room. Michaelson closed the door quietly; stood with his back to it.

One of the three men—a big man in an overcoat—got up from the rickety chair on which he was sitting.

He said: "Gestapo!"

Duborg said: "Do you have to tell us? From my earliest days I was trained to smell rats."

The big man smiled. It was not an unpleasant smile. His face and head were almost square; his hair close-cropped. His eyes were of a peculiar pale blue colour. He said, almost casually:

"You are Henri Francois Duborg, and you—" jerking his thumb towards Michaelson—"are George Ernest Michaelson. You are agents in the pay of the British Government. You are civilians and therefore entitled to be shot. It is possible that a more lenient view may be taken of your case if you decide to talk."

Michaelson said quietly: "Nuts to you!"

The big man shrugged his shoulders. He said: "It really doesn't matter if you don't. Because Cerisette Mavrique decided to talk this afternoon."

Duborg said: "I bet you had to make her."

The big man nodded. "Believe me, my friend," he said, "she was very difficult, but she talked eventually. You know, we have ways."

Duborg said: "You're telling me! But I would like to tell you this—" He stepped forward. He kicked the German in the pit of the stomach.

The big man shrieked. He fell to the floor; lay there writhing. After a minute he began to whimper.

The man in the corner with the Mauser pistol raised the lower part of his arm. He fired three shots. Each shot hit Duborg in the stomach.

The second man, who was still seated, got up slowly. He put his hand in his pocket. As he moved, Michaelson shot across the room in something that looked like a rugby tackle. They went on to the floor in a heap. Michaelson had one thumb in the Gestapo man's eye. The man with the pistol in the corner of the room was unable to do anything about it. He stood there, the pistol ready, looking vaguely annoyed; a little uncomfortable. The big man had stopped whimpering. He was huddled in the corner of the room, holding his stomach. Duborg was dead.

Michaelson took his thumb out of his opponent's eye; slipped his hand down to his throat. The movement allowed the man in the corner to get a shot. He took careful aim. He shot Michaelson through the head. The man underneath Michaelson put up his arm and pushed the body away from him. He got up. He leaned against the wall, breathing heavily.

The man with the pistol said in German: "This will be considered to be very unsatisfactory. We were supposed to bring these two in."

The man leaning against the wall said: "These cursed spies— they always do this sort of thing!" He began to brush his clothes. "And why not?"

The man with the pistol nodded. He said: "This is the easiest way for them." He went over to the big man; looked down at him. He said: "They have hurt Karl very badly. I should think he will always remember them."

On the corner of the street, the white-faced boy, Carlos, stood. His face made a white blot in the miasma of the fog. When he heard the shots he turned. He began to walk quickly down the hill towards the Place des Roses, towards Fours' wine shop.

II

Presenting Mr. Quayle. If the introduction is mainly pictorial it is because few people were privileged to know the ramifications of the mind of Mr. Quayle. Sometimes he was not quite certain about them himself. He lived, from a mental angle, as far ahead as was possible, mainly because the people who were dependent upon his peculiar mentality lived, usually, from moment to moment, sometimes dying even more suddenly than that.

If these processes had brought a certain acid outlook, a certain jaundiced viewpoint of the world—and the men and women in it—to him, he might be easily forgiven. There are things worse than bad temper.

He was tall, limber, well-made. He dressed quietly. He had a *flair* for not being too noticeable in crowds, for remaining a part of the scenery and, as such, not attracting too much attention. This was only one of his many attributes, which was as well, for the peculiar profession to which he belonged demanded many qualities and a great deal of extremely stark determination.

He paid off the cab, went through the swing doors into the Hyde Park Hotel, through the outer *foyer*, paused at the cloak-room, left his overcoat and his black Homburg hat; went into the Buttery. The place was crowded. It was filled with British and American officers, members of the Women's Services; all sorts and conditions of people.

Quayle sat on a high stool at the end of the bar. He ordered a double gin and soda, thinking as he did so that it was a depressing drink, but that in any event life could scarcely be more depressing than it was at the moment.

The top of his head was bald. A fringe of hair gave him the appearance of a tonsured monk. His face was round and might be called either very intelligent or vaguely stupid, according to the way he desired it to look. He sat there, sipping the gin and soda, looking straight in front of him.

Life, thought Quayle, was rather ridiculous—tragically ridiculous. Definitely, that was an adequate description of life at this particular moment. He threw a sidelong glance to his left—a glance which embraced the attractive picture of a young woman in W.R.N.S. uniform, whose neatly dressed blonde hair under an attractive tricorn uniform hat, her well-developed bosom, flat stomach and good legs, gave Quayle for one fleeting second a respite from the annoyance that thronged his mind—then brought his eyes back to the line of bottles on the mirrored shelves in front of him.

Quayle's business was nobody's business. That is the best description of his profession. It was a business necessitated by war, by the ghastly mechanics of war, by the scheming, plotting, machinations, underhand tactics, filthy murders; all those things that go to make up modern Armageddon, which is not entirely composed of battles in the air and clashes between infantry.

He finished the gin, ordered another. He took a large cigarette case from his pocket, extracted a cigarette, lit it, began to smoke. He was impatient.

A long and dangerous life had taught Quayle that there are only certain things which one is really afraid of—a certain kind of situation, a certain type of woman. One is afraid of both these things for the same reason. Both the situation and the woman are uncertain. They may repercuss in ways unforeseen. The situation, not being known, may possess potentialities for annoyance. The woman, whether she be known or not, may develop characteristics undreamed of. These were dangerous things one might sometimes be afraid of. The other and possibly more important thing was the amazing fretfulness of indecision, the inability to make up one's mind to deal with a situation because there are no facts on which one *can* make up one's mind; the appalling inability to realise the basis of the picture; the pressing desire to seize on small clues, to build up something in order that one might do something—*anything*—knowing all the time that if one *did* do something it would probably be wrong because the basic facts were missing.

The man who said "when in doubt don't" knew what he was talking about. He probably guessed, too, just how badly most people needed that advice.

Quayle was what might be described as a very tough egg. Yet he had a house just outside London, a wife who was devoted to him, and who believed—strange as it may seem—that he was employed in some quite normal department of a Ministry. He had all the attributes, the background, of a normal upper-middle class Englishman who was nearly fifty years of age, who was a little perturbed with the war because it interfered with his life, who was like so many people of his type that one sees about the streets. Yet he was none of these things.

A dangerous man—a fearful man—Quayle; a man at whose bidding strange things happened in many parts of the world; a man who ordered death and hated it; a man who pulled strings and made puppets dance; who whilst pulling the strings came near to weeping—if he *could* come near to weeping—because the puppets *had* to dance. This was Quayle.

A man came into the Buttery, through the *foyer*. He was a big, broad-shouldered man, with a big, good-looking face. He wore battledress, with a Commando flash under the shoulder title "Canada." A little inclined to stoutness, but his uniform sat well on him. His ankles and feet were trim; his hands, large, with spatulate fingers, hung at the end of long arms relaxed and limp.

Imperceptibly Quayle moved a little to the right, and the Canadian, as imperceptibly, inserted himself into the space made for him. Quayle ordered another large gin and soda. He drank half of it, stubbed out his cigarette, selected a fresh one from his case. He produced a lighter from his pocket which failed to work. He said to the Canadian:

"Could you give me a light?"

The Canadian grinned. Looking at him one could sense that he was a happy man; that in most circumstances—even the most difficult ones—he would still be happy.

He said: "Yeah, I got a light." He produced a lighter from his pocket, snapped it on, bent towards Quayle, showing the Captain's stars on his shoulders. He said, as he held the flame to Quayle's cigarette: "Do I talk?"

Quayle nodded. "It's all right," he said. "Talk."

Dombie said: "I went around to the office, but you weren't there. I saw the girl. She said she reckoned you'd be here. I reckon you've been waitin' to see me for some time, hey?"

Quayle said in a bored voice: "Have I?" The fingers of his right hand were tapping impatiently under the ledge of the bar.

Dombie went on: "I know how it's been. I guess you haven't been having a good time. O.K. Well, it's bloody awful some more. It looks like they've done it again."

Quayle said: "God damn it!" There was a world of feeling in the words.

"You're tellin' me," said Dombie. "Where do we go from here?"

The white-jacketed barman, passing along the bar, stood in front of them. Dombie said cheerfully:

"Hey, fella, you got whisky? I'll take a large one with just a little soda. Make it snappy, pal." He put a pound note on the counter. The barman went away.

Quayle said: "What happened and where did you get it from?"

The Canadian eased his large backside on the stool. He brought out a leather cigarette case, extracted a Lucky Strike, lit it. He was cool, unperturbed. He said:

"Through Fours' place. Believe it or not, I was over there last night. I got picked up by a plane at Frenduly in the Pas de Calais. I got over here this morning. Christ—was I glad to get out of there?"

Quayle said: "It's hot, is it?"

Dombie grinned. "Hot? It's a bloody cauldron," he said. "Jerry's worried. You know what the Germans are like when they get frightened, don't you? They get so tough it hurts. If they're doubtful they start killin'."

Quayle said: "Go on."

Dombie said: "All right. It reads like this. That musical comedy Vichy police force got wise to Michaelson and Duborg. You got that? They knocked off Mavrique. She was the contact with those two. Yet it wouldn't have been so bad if they'd handled her. But they didn't. They handed her over to the black coat brigade—one of the Gestapo inner sections. I reckon they made little Cerisette talk plenty. They got some nice methods, you know."

Quayle said: "You don't have to tell me. I know." His tone was angry.

Dombie said: "She shot the works. Duborg and Michaelson met at Fours' shop. They went home. They guessed what was waiting for 'em and got that kid Carlos—a white-faced rat but a nice guy—to come on behind to see what happened. O.K. There was a show-down. The Gestapo boys were waiting for Duborg and Michaelson. It looks like there was a rough-house. Our two boys got creased. That's all there is to it. They sent round a mortuary wagon and brought 'em out." He sighed. "Those two didn't talk anyway."

Quayle said in an angry low voice: "You bet your goddamned life they didn't talk, Dombie. Whatever they'd have done to them they'd never have talked."

The Canadian said: "Yeah, I guess you're right. I reckon that's where they started something. They weren't going to take a chance on talking. Those two boys knew what these guys do to a fella when they really want to find out something." He grinned. "You're tellin' me!" he said.

Quayle finished his gin and soda. He sucked down the clear liquid angrily. He pushed the glass back across the bar. The barman approached. Quayle ordered fresh drinks. Underneath the ledge of the bar the fingers of his right hand were still tapping.

Dombie said: "Look, Mr. Quayle, take it easy. I know how you're feelin'. You send 'em out there and you wish you were with 'em. Well, you can't be. None of these boys have taken as many chances as you have."

Quayle said: "I don't give a damn about Duborg and Michaelson. If they had to have it they had to have it. That's the way it goes." His voice sank to a low sibilant whisper. There was a world of hatred in every syllable. He said: "I want to know who gave the woman away. How did those dressed-up Vichy fools get on to Mavrique? How did they know about her?"

Dombie spread the fingers of his right hand on the top of the bar. The palm looked like a small plate. The fingers, short, spatulate, with broad nails, spread themselves out. Vaguely, they reminded Quayle of an octopus who had had his tentacles cut short.

Dombie said: "Look, whatever trouble started with Mavrique started over here. There are too many of these goddam Jerries kickin' around. You know that. Some of 'em are being let kick around. They give 'em their heads. Other departments believe if you give 'em enough rope they'll hang themselves."

Quayle said: "*I've* never believed that."

Dombie shrugged his shoulders. He said: "Mr. Quayle, there's only one man could know about Mavrique; there's only one man who could have tipped those bastards off, and you know who he is."

Quayle said: "Yes, I know. That would be Lelley."

Dombie looked round the Buttery. It was almost empty. It was nearly ten o'clock. He said:

"That's right. It would be Lelley. I'd like to tear him wide open." An idea came to him. "Listen," he said, "why don't I tear him wide open?"

Quayle said: "That's not *your* business." He smiled. "You're good at your job, Dombie, but that's not your line." There was a pause. He went on: "You're right. You've got to be right. It was our friend Mr. Charles Ermyn Lelley. Otherwise little Fritzy—that superb product of Mr. Himmler's No. 1 Training School—Mr. Lelley of Upper Nelswood—the squire of the village."

Dombie said: "He could have done it. He was the only guy who could have done it. We know he knew about Mavrique. When they let her get through the first time and come over here he knew about it. I'm tellin' you!"

Quayle said: "I know that."

Dombie said: "It's not good over there. You know they've been knocking off our contacts like hell. They got eleven of them in the last five months, Mr. Quayle."

Quayle said: "I know." His voice was almost harsh.

Dombie said: "But we keep on sending 'em because— goddam it—we've got to keep on sending them. We've got to know the way things are. You said that, you know, Mr. Quayle."

Quayle smiled. He said: "I know. I've a way out of that. I'm going to draw a line across the whole organisation we've got over there. I'm bringing every contact back. That's going to fix them."

Dombie said: "That's clever. What are you doing—sending a new lot out?"

Quayle nodded. "I'm sending seventeen people they'll never know. Seventeen people *they'll* never know—seventeen people that Mr. Lelley will never know about."

The Canadian said: "I hope Lelley don't have a chance of knowing about 'em. He's a clever bastard and he's got some sort of contact across the Irish Channel. He gets it back to France somehow."

Quayle looked at Dombie. He smiled. Dombie began to feel happy. He knew that smile.

Quayle said: "Lelley's not going to know about the seventeen who are going over. He won't have the chance."

Dombie said: "I'm glad to hear it." He finished his drink. He said: "Will you have another?"

Quayle nodded.

Dombie ordered the drinks. When they were brought, and the barman gone, Quayle said:

"They were nice boys, those two. Duborg—he was something like you, and Michaelson was a sound fellow. I trained him. I had him working for me for five years. He'd been everywhere and done everything. It's a tough way to finish."

Dombie said: "I reckon there are worse ways. I reckon he did something to 'em before they fogged him."

They drank their drinks.

Quayle got off the stool. He said: "I'm going to do some telephoning. Take a couple of days off. Come and see me in two or three days' time. You know where."

Dombie said: "O.K., boss. I'll be seein' you." He got off the stool. He went on: "I'm glad you made up your mind about Lelley. I think it's a good thing."

Quayle said nothing.

He walked out of the Buttery, got his hat and coat at the cloakroom, went away.

The Canadian lit a fresh cigarette; ordered some more whisky. He stood there looking into the mirror in front of him. Reflected, he could see the faces of men and women seated in the bar. Dombie, who was of an amatory disposition, examined carefully the faces and figures of the women, amused himself by considering which one he would sleep with if he had the choice.

He sat down on the high stool and drank the whisky slowly. It tasted good. He reflected on life. Yesterday evening he had been in France—occupied France—waiting for the plane that would come down inside the box barrage of bombs dropped by the co-operative Squadrons, the plane that would, if all were well, pick him up. Well . . . it had come. He had been picked up. He was here. Dombie grinned. He'd been over there, dropped and picked up, twenty-two times. One of these fine days something was going to slip-up and he'd probably be for the high jump too—like Duborg and Michaelson.

He finished his drink; winked at the bar-tender, got another one.

He sat there wondering what he should do next—where he should go.

Life, thought Dombie, was O.K.

It was O.K. all right if you didn't weaken.

III

Kerr leaned on the top of the grand piano; regarded the slender fingers of Therese Martyr as they glided over the piano keys. She played softly, with a superb technique. She imbued the hot number with a certain musical quality which had certainly not existed in the mind of its composer.

Therese was tall, slim, vital. She had long narrow feet. By moving his head a little Kerr could see her feet on the piano pedals. Therese, he thought, was very beautiful below the waist.

She had flat breasts, a long and rather mournful face. Her eyes were beautiful, and she had a definite and peculiar appeal.

Kerr looked at the reflection of his face in the polished piano-case. He thought: I wonder—are you slightly drunk or merely a little excited? He wished he knew. It was rather difficult to know when you were getting a little high. Kerr had spent a great many years of his life drinking; being unaffected by the process. But these days you didn't know. You weren't certain.

The room was "L" shaped. The walls and ceiling were painted off-white. They glistened. The lighting was cleverly concealed in old Spanish iron sconces. The parquet floor was black and polished. It had black and white rugs on it. The two long windows, one on each side of the "L", were covered with off-white brocade curtains, with their borders illuminated by a raised black and gold motif. Kerr thought it was a hell of a flat. It was one of those places. It had everything—comfort, taste; and the women were always good too. Any woman who came to Mrs. Milton's parties seemed to be beautiful in some way or another. Or was she? Kerr wondered whether it was *he* who made them beautiful; whether it was because he was usually happy at Glynda's parties; whether he was really happy or whether he was just a little drunk?

Kerr raised his head, looked across the room. Sandra was leaning against the wall directly opposite him. She was dressed in a long, superbly cut, dinner frock in some soft, clinging material the colour of bluebells. Round her neck and right wrist she wore handsome antique gilt jewellery set with semi-precious stones.

She had honey-coloured hair, luminous violet eyes. She was high-breasted, slim-hipped. She was quite lovely.

Kerr grinned at her. He said to himself: You've got a lovely wife. You've got a hell of a wife. She's quite wonderful!

She smiled at him without moving. She stood absolutely still, smiling at him, looking unutterably beautiful. Quietly and unutterably beautiful.

Kerr thought that Sandra was always relaxed. No matter what happened, she always appeared to be relaxed, quiet. Yet really, underneath, she was not. Definitely not.

He picked up the glass that was near him, gulped down some whisky; leaned again on the piano top. He began to think about Sandra. He told himself that it was a very good thing for a man to think objectively about his wife on occasion. When he looked up she was still leaning against the wall, still smiling, still watching him.

In the corner, holding a long straight glass and talking to the Spaniard—Miguales, was Glynda Milton—a brunette, slim, with tiny feet and hands; wearing a short red dress—gesticulating a little wildly with her free hand. Kerr thought: Glynda's a little high. But I think everybody at this party is high. Except Sandra. Sandra never gets high.

Kerr was tall, slim, good-looking: tough-looking. He had a peculiar attraction—something that was indefinable; something that made women like him. He knew this. He had good shoulders, slim hips. He was long-legged. His hands were strong, artistic hands. His hair was dark brown and waved a little. He was one of those men whose clothes are always right.

He began to watch Therese's fingers again. She was playing something else now. He didn't know what the tune was called but it had allure—definitely it had allure. Kerr thought that allure was an extremely attractive word. He liked it. He liked it so much he repeated it to himself two or three times.

He looked round the room. Glynda was by now even more involved in her argument with the Spaniard. Sitting on the long white brocade settee, Magdalen Francis talked in her soft and attractive voice to a Fighting French officer. Kerr listened to her. One could always listen to the cadences of Magdalen's voice. It was soothing. She wore a pale green frock—a very expensive affair—and her blonde hair was supremely dressed. Magdalen always looked as if she had just stepped out of a band-box. She had style.

Kerr came to the conclusion that he wouldn't drink any more. He thought it would be a hell of a good idea not to drink any more. One or two more and he was likely to begin thinking in terms of just what he could try out with some of the women. And that wouldn't do at all.

Therese got up from the piano. She went to the upper part of the room and began to talk to Elvira Fayle. Kerr thought they made a great picture, those two; talking together, smiling at each other. Therese made a picture. In spite of her flat breasts she made a hell of a picture. She knew how to dress, that one. She wore a long black skirt with a most lovely cream lace blouse. Her dark hair was swept back high from her face. Elvira, who was almost plain, but with good feet and legs and a peculiar grace, swayed a little as she talked. Elvira had been hitting the gin again, Kerr thought. She liked gin. She liked gin and poker and watching other people get drunk. The trouble was that she invariably got drunk first. She obtained the most beautiful *lingerie* from somebody in the Black Market because, as she put it, other people were always putting her to bed. Kerr thought she was a nice dish.

They were, all of them, rather attractive women. He thought that most of them had all the things that women ought to have. He wondered just how much each woman knew or thought about him in conjunction with the rest of them. He wondered . . .

He began to wonder about Sandra. It would be funny if she got wise to him. Or was she wise—about the women, he meant? Of course she wasn't wise about the other thing. God, thought Kerr, if she knew about the other thing. . . . Well, she would forgive anything he did. She might even think he was a hero.

What *did* she think? Possibly that he was drinking a little too much; that he was taking advantage of the quite soft job he had—that specially earmarked and reserved job in that Government Department, which existed merely on paper to supply *alibis* for people like Kerr.

Therese came back to the piano. She said: "Ricky, what do you want me to play?"

He looked at her. She had violet shadows under her cheekbones and her mouth was raspberry.

He said: "What would you like to play to me, Sweetie-pie?"

She looked at him for a long time; then she smiled slowly.

She said very softly, almost under her breath: "If I played what I *ought* to play I'd play '*I'll be glad when you're dead, you rascal you.*'"

Kerr said: "But you don't really mean that, do you?"

She looked at him impertinently. She said: "Why not?" She began to play some piece which he didn't recognise but which he liked. Maybe she knew the sort of music he went for. She *ought* to know anyway.

Quayle opened the door of his flat; went into the hallway. He switched on the light, closed the door behind him, stood uncertainly, his hands in his overcoat pockets. He was thinking about Lelley. Rather grimly Quayle considered Lelley's background. After a few moments he shrugged his shoulders; took off his overcoat. He walked across the hall, down the long passageway into the kitchen. He opened the scullery door, then the door of what seemed to be a cupboard on the far side of the scullery. He passed through into the flat next door. He walked down the passageway, turned into the second door on the left. The room was furnished as an office. The walls were lined with steel filing cabinets. There was a double desk in the centre of the room with five telephones on it, each marked with a numbered disc. On one side of the desk a blonde girl in the uniform of a Squadron Officer in the W.A.A.F. politely stifled a yawn with a white hand.

Quayle said: "Good-evening, Myra. Where's Cordover?"

She said at once: "He's been off for three weeks. He's at home. He rang through and reported this evening. He sounded as if he were going to bed. Do you want him?"

Quayle said: "Not for the moment. Give me the Lelley file."

She got up, went to one of the steel cabinets, opened it, flipped through the dozens of tightly packed folders inside. She gave one to Quayle. He sat down on the other side of the desk, looked at the folder. It said:

"Charles Ermyn Lelley—originally Enrique Luis, with Norwegian papers, reputed to be the owner of a small shipping line working along the Scandinavian coast between there and Scottish ports—noted by M.I.5. in 1935 as possible enemy agent. January 1939 as Diomede Falza, with Czech papers, working in newspaper offices and generally throughout Czecho-Slovakia. Direct contact traced with Himmler organisation. June 1939 England—Nelswood. Bought the local Manor estate. Subscribed heavily to local funds. Reputed to be the third son of Jonathan Lelley (this son had been abroad for some fifteen years).

"Traced as contact between German Embassy London 1939 and Himmler organisation. Main contacts in Eire. Uses original and undiscovered 'post-office' system.

"General Record: Was employed in Gestapo Investigations Department, Colombia House, Berlin. Organised original anti-Jew riots for S.A. Considered to be a sadist.

"Speaks perfectly, English, German, French, Spanish, Portuguese. Has been operating from Nelswood since 1939."

Then followed a pencilled question mark.

Quayle stood looking at the typescript in front of him. His expression was almost benign. He said to the blonde girl:

"Have you a cigarette, Myra?"

She nodded. She went to a leather handbag, produced a cigarette, gave it to him.

Quayle lit it. He smoked silently; then he threw the folder across the table. He said:

"You can mark the Lelley record closed, and you can put it away in the 'Concluded' file."

She said: "Yes, Mr. Quayle. You mean 'no further action'?"

Quayle smiled at her. He said: "I mean 'no further action.' "

He leaned back in his chair, drew on his cigarette. He said: "Are they all back?"

"All except two, Mr. Quayle," she said. "We lost two."

Quayle nodded. He asked: "Casualties?"

The girl said: "They were killed. We don't know how or where."

Quayle said: "And the other nine are back?"

"All back," she said. She looked at Quayle. She was considering what he was going to do.

Quayle said: "Do you know where Kerr is?"

She said: "No, I don't. You remember his last job was with Cordover. That means they'd both be on leave. Cordover would know where he was."

Quayle said: "All right. Get through to Cordover. Tell him to stand by. I shall be telephoning him some time—some time to-night. Tell Cordover to be certain he knows where Kerr is."

She said: "Very well, Mr. Quayle."

Quayle got up. He stood, the cigarette in the fingers of his left hand, looking at her. He said:

"This is the hell of a game, isn't it, Myra?"

She nodded. "You're telling me," she said. "It's all right for me. I only take messages."

Quayle said. "I'm going to rest for an hour. Then I'll tell you what I want done. I'll probably want to speak to Cordover."

She said: "Very well, Mr. Quayle."

Quayle went out of the room, went back to his own flat. He switched on the electric fire in the bedroom, stood looking at it. He was thinking about Lelley.

Lelley had asked for it and by God he was going to get it! Quayle began to pace up and down the bedroom, drawing on the cigarette. *Now* he was certain about Lelley. When Mavrique had been over five weeks ago Lelley had been on to her. He had used the Hungarian "refugee" who occasionally worked for him. He'd had a tail on her for days. Everyone was rather amused at that. Even he, Quayle, had wondered what the hell Lelley had thought he was playing at. And then Mavrique had gone back to France and Vichy had got on to her and handed her over. The only person who could have let them have information about Mavrique was Lelley. He'd done it *somehow*.

Probably through the German group in Eire. Anyhow he'd done it, and Mavrique and Duborg and Michaelson were finished and probably Fours and the boy Carlos would eventually get it too. Quayle wondered just how much Mavrique had talked. Just who she had put away . . . poor little so-and-so.

He shrugged his shoulders, took off his coat, waistcoat and shoes. He lay down on the bed, put his hands behind his head, lay looking at the ceiling, working out details.

IV

Sammy Cordover opened his eyes, stretched, looked at the ceiling. The ceiling was mottled. It presented to his eyes a design which for some reason perturbed him. His mouth was dry. He ran his tongue over his lips; considered that when he woke up at this time his mouth was always dry.

Through the top of the window the fog came into the room. He could taste it. One of those London fogs which came suddenly for no rhyme or reason, and which were associated in his mind with unpleasant things.

He raised his head. At the bottom of the bed he could see one large toe sticking out from the bedclothes, reminding him vaguely that life was a practical and unpleasant thing.

The room was small, badly furnished, untidy. In the corner, on a chair, were his clothes. The rather wide and knife-creased trousers, folded carefully, and the double-breasted, high and tight-waisted, coat, with the padded shoulders. Beneath the chair—in Woolworth trees—were his shoes, pointed-toed, polished. Sammy was smart all right. That's what the girls thought. A clever boy, Sammy. He made good money working for an out-of-town Transport Company, and he knew how to spend it. A snappy dresser. And nice and quiet. He never took a liberty . . . well . . . not so you'd notice it. Generous too. . . . That's what they thought.

He put his head back on the pillow and relaxed. He wished something would happen. It was all very well, this hanging around, spending a few quid and having a good time. It was O.K. But it wasn't particularly satisfying. Not that anything was particularly satisfying . . . Still, now and then there was a bit of excitement . . . just a little bit. . . . . He grinned.

Sammy Cordover was a Cockney. He belonged to that unique, that supreme, tribe of people who being born and having their being in London, are imbued with all those qualities, and defects, that go to make up the London Cockney. He was tough.

He was twenty-seven years of age. In those twenty-seven years he had experienced most of those things that fall to the lot of a person who, brought up in London, forced to pit himself against the mentality of the great City, had become tough, clever and cunning in the process. He was a worshipper of things which he considered to be better than he was—things which, although he wouldn't have put it in those words, possessed quality.

He yawned. He continued to look at the ceiling, to go through, to consider, the last few years of his life. Like most of the people of his class who are, in their own peculiar way, aristocratic to a degree unknown to some ladies and gentlemen who possess family trees, Sammy possessed the quality of believing that the things he did were right because he considered that they were right. He lived on this belief. He had unfailing faith in the rightness of the people who told him what to do. He had this faith because he believed in them. God damn it—you had to believe in something!

He reached out his hand, took a cigarette from the packet of Players on the table at his elbow, lit it with a showy green and gold lighter. He began to smoke. He wondered how long he was to be allowed to remain walking about the city, spending the adequate money which was paid to him on the first of each month, drinking half-pints of beer out of pewter mugs in strange public houses, waiting for something to happen.

He wondered about his future. He wondered what happened to a man who did the sort of work he did; what future there was. He realised that whatever lay ahead, whatever ordinary routine of work might come to him in the years before him, would be tinged by what he was doing now. Life would never be the same as it had been before the war. He doubted whether it would even be worth while.

He got out of bed. He was naked. He stood in the middle of the floor; a thin, not too well-developed specimen, yet strong and supple, with large feet, bony knees, a thin body. His face was long and thin, his nose large. Beneath a shock of black hair, a good forehead, above clear luminous eyes, gave him a certain appearance of intellectuality.

He stood there in the middle of the cheap dusty room, smoking the cigarette, wondering what he was going to do.

The telephone, incongruously modern in such a place, began to jangle. He went over to the mantelpiece, took the receiver off the hook.

He said in a quiet nasal voice: "This is Cordover."

The blonde girl's voice came softly over the telephone. She said: "Good-night to you. Hold on, please. I'm connecting you . . ."

He said: "O.K. I'm listenin'."

Quayle's voice came quietly and clearly. It said: "Good-evening, Sammy. This is Quayle. Where's Mr. Kerr?"

Sammy moved the cigarette from one side of his mouth to the other. He said: "He's at a party—at Mrs. Milton's place. She's a friend of Mrs. Kerr's. He told me he was going there to-night. I've got the number. He'll be there now."

Quayle said: "All right. Ring through to him. Tell him to meet me in the usual place. Tell him he's to be there at twelve-thirty. I want to talk to him. There's a little job for both of you to-night. I think he'd like to have you with him."

Sammy grinned into the mouthpiece. He said: "O.K., Mr. Quayle."

Quayle said: "You tell him to meet me. Then you wait for him to get in touch with you. You understand that?"

Sammy said: "I get it, Mr. Quayle. I'll get through to him at once."

Quayle said: "All right. So long, Sammy."

Cordover said so long. He hung up the receiver, stood looking at the telephone. The cigarette had gone out and hung limply on to his lip.

He turned away. He began to grin as if he had just thought of something amusing.

Somewhere in the flat a clock struck twelve. It had a resonant, tinny, note.

Close to him, as he leaned against the wall near the doorway, Kerr could see the face of Magdalen Francis. He thought vaguely that he went for Magdalen quite a lot.

She came near to him. She said: "Ricky, I think you're tight, and I think you're awfully nice when you're tight."

He smiled at her. He said: "Don't you believe that. Drink brings out the worst in me. I'm a fearful fellow."

She laughed. Her laughter rippled delightfully. It came from somewhere at the back of her throat.

She said: "Of course you are. All the best people are cads, Ricky. But then *I* don't mind your being cut. You carry your liquor very well. No one would know."

He looked at her sideways. "So they wouldn't know?" he said. "Just fancy that, Sweet. And *what* wouldn't they know?"

She looked at him. It seemed to Kerr that she was looking at him for an awfully long time. It seemed to him that in her eyes he could read almost a story—an amusing story. Suddenly her face became serious—just for a second; then she smiled again.

She said: "If I know anything about you they wouldn't know anything you didn't want them to know."

He said: "So you think I'm like that, Magdalen?"

She said: "Well, aren't you?"

Out of the corner of his eye he could see Sandra. Sandra was standing by the end of the settee. She was talking to Miguales.

Magdalen said something, but Kerr did not hear. He was not listening. He was watching Miguales.

There was no doubt about it, the Spaniard had something— definitely! He was tall, lithe. His face was thin, clean-cut and bronzed. Miguales was a scrapper all right. As far as Kerr could make out he'd fought on both sides in the Spanish Civil War and enjoyed the process. He seemed to be impartial about revolutions. He had a quiet, definite, sense of humour. He was tough. Kerr, looking at Miguales, subconsciously hearing the soft sounds that emanated from Miguales' mouth, thought that the Spaniard could be *very* tough if he wanted to be. But his voice was soft. His hands, contradicting his face, were white. The fingers were long and supple. Women went for Miguales— too damned much, thought Kerr. He wondered what Sandra thought about him.

He moved. He stretched his shoulders. He said to Magdalen: "Go on, Sweet, I love to hear you talking." He continued to think about the Spaniard.

The question was, thought Kerr, whether Sandra could ever go for anybody. He doubted it. He doubted it very much. Kerr had the supreme egotism of an individual who had spent his life in thinking in terms of himself, because he had been forced to think in terms of himself; because most of his life he had been coming to conclusions—tough ones. Because it had become necessary for him to make decisions—tough decisions; to act quickly—spontaneously. If you are like that you have to be an egotist. Of course it goes without saying that Kerr did not know he was one. No true egotist ever realises the fact.

He thought about Sandra. Sandra was always nice to every-body. And she was being nice to Miguales because he was lonely, unhappy and without money—a neutral living in a country that was too concerned with a big-time war to have much time to worry about the finances—the heartaches—of neutrals. The idea came to Kerr that one of these fine days when he felt like it he would have a talk with Sandra. He would try and find out something about this well-poised, relaxed, entirely charming and delightful woman who was his wife—a woman who could be passionate and yet maintain even during moments of passion a certain reserve which was as delightful as it was unexpected. One of these days, thought Kerr, he must certainly talk to her.

Magdalen was saying very quietly, with a party smile masking the expression in her eyes: "You haven't telephoned me, Ricky. You haven't telephoned me for days. What about it?"

He smiled. When he smiled his face was quite illuminated. Then he looked quite handsome. He said:

"You don't say! What's going on around here? Just fancy my not having telephoned you!"

She said under her breath: "Quiet, Ricky. Don't be a damned fool."

He said, as quietly: "Why not? We're all fools, Magdalen. You're one—so am I. Aren't we all?"

She shrugged one shoulder petulantly. She said: "Possibly—but do we have to tell the whole damned world about it?"

Kerr said: "I wouldn't know. But then I wouldn't know anything." He felt that he wanted to go somewhere; flop in a big chair; relax. He felt tired.

Somewhere in the flat a telephone began to ring. The noise of the telephone bell grated on Kerr's nerves. The ringing of the bell seemed imbued with a peculiar harshness. Magdalen Francis moved away from him. She moved down the room and round into the other end of the "L." Kerr stood there by himself, leaning against the wall, with the butt end of a cigarette beginning to burn his fingers.

Glynda Milton came into the room from the hallway. She said:

"Ricky, you're wanted on the telephone."

Kerr said: "Thanks, Glynda." Strangely enough, he was not at all surprised. Subconsciously, he'd felt that the telephone message would be for him. He'd been sticking around doing nothing for too long. Maybe something was going to break. He moved out of the room, along the passageway, into the hallway. He moved quickly and surely. If he were drunk he did not show it. He looked round the hall before he took up the receiver, made certain he was alone.

He said: "Hallo! This is Kerr."

Sammy Cordover's voice came over the line. He said: "Good-evening, Mr. Kerr. Or maybe I ought to say good-morning. This is Sammy."

Kerr said: "Yes. So what?"

Cordover said: "The old man's been talkin' to me. He wants you to see him."

Kerr said: "Yes, of course. When?"

Sammy Cordover said: "Now. He's burned up about something. You're to see him right away. He told me to stand by."

Kerr felt a little spasm in his stomach as if someone had put a tight hand on the muscles—a nervous thing. He wished he hadn't drunk quite so much.

He said: "All right. As usual, I suppose?"

Sammy Cordover said: "Yes, as usual. I s'pose I'll be hearin' from you, Mr. Kerr?"

Kerr said: "Yes. I'll get in touch with you when I know what's what. So long."

He hung up the receiver.

He stood for a moment looking at the telephone. He thought that telephones were extraordinary things. They rang; you received a message. Promptly you became somebody else. You had to do something. His nerves stretched; then tautened. He felt quite sober.

He turned away from the telephone, crossed the hall. He began to walk along the passage. Half-way along, on an antique chest, he saw his hat. He picked it up. Sandra came out of the drawing-room. She came towards him; stopped a few feet from him. Kerr thought she looked unutterably lovely.

She said: "Was she nice to you, Ricky?"

He grinned at her. He asked: "What do you mean—was she nice? Did you think I was talking to a woman?"

She smiled. He watched her mouth as she smiled. He loved to see the shape of her lips break; to see her white teeth gleam.

"Of course it was a woman. It must be. You don't mean to tell me that somebody's ringing you on business at this time of night?"

He said: "Sandra, you're quite wrong. In fact that was the Ministry."

She laughed—a delightful laugh. She made a little gurgling sound in her throat. She said:

"Like hell it was, Ricky! It was some woman. And you've got your hat in your hand. She must be a wonderful woman to get you away from this party, because there're some awfully nice ones here."

Kerr said: "There's one wonderful one here."

She laughed again. She said: "Meaning me, Sir?"

Kerr said: "Meaning you."

There was a pause. She said: "I suppose I shall be seeing you some time?"

"Of course," said Kerr. "I shall probably see you to-morrow morning. This is just one of those things. You know, there's a war on, Sandra."

She nodded. "Somebody told me about that. Good-night, Ricky dear." She turned; went back into the drawing-room.

Kerr looked at his hat. It was a nice hat, he thought—a nice tobacco coloured hat. He liked it. He went to the door of the drawing-room. Just round the corner he could see Glynda.

He said: " 'Bye, Glynda. Thank you for a lovely party. Don't think I haven't enjoyed myself, because I haven't. Bless you, darling."

She said: " 'Bye, Ricky. I don't know where you're going to, but wherever it is don't do anything that I wouldn't like to hear about."

Kerr turned away. As he turned, he had a last glimpse of Sandra. She was in the far corner of the room. She had gone back to Miguales.

A cold wind was blowing. Kerr passed the St. James's Theatre and turned down into Pall Mall Place. He looked at his watch. It was twelve-thirty. Half-way down the narrow alleyway was a small, dark blue door, sandwiched between the houses on each side. Kerr took a key from his pocket; opened the door, closed it behind him. He took a small flash-lamp out of his pocket, switched it on, walked up the narrow wooden stairway. He opened the door on the right of the first landing.

The room was a small square room, furnished with a desk and a few chairs. Quayle, smoking a cigarette, sat behind the desk.

He said: "Good-evening, Ricky."

Kerr said: "Good-evening." He stood, a cigarette in his mouth, his hands in his pockets, regarding Quayle with casual equanimity.

Quayle said: "Did you have a good party?"

Kerr said: "Not too bad."

Quayle sighed. He said: "I used to be a bit of a party hound myself in the old days. I don't get much time now."

Kerr said: "I shouldn't think you get very much time for anything. Do you ever go to sleep?"

"Not often," said Quayle evenly. "I don't sleep too well these days." He got up. He threw his cigarette end into the fireplace.

He said: "It's like this: We're having a lot of trouble over the other side. They got on to one of my people—a woman. They made her talk. That's not very good."

Kerr said: "No, that wouldn't be."

Quayle went on: "There's only one way to play that. I've brought the people we've been using back. We've been pretty lucky about that. We've only lost two in the process. I'm going to send out a new lot."

Kerr nodded. "A good idea," he said. "There's nothing like a clean sweep."

Quayle said. "I know. But there's a snag."

Kerr waited patiently to hear how all this concerned him.

Quayle went on: "There's a man over here, out at Nelswood. He's supposed to be Charles Ermyn Lelley. He lives in the Manor House there. He's been there some time. He's one of their star people. We've let him run around for a long time because one or two of the Service Intelligence Departments thought that might be a good thing to do."

He shrugged his shoulders. "The time has come," he said, "when I think it's going to be a very bad thing to do. I'm not going to have it."

Kerr said nothing.

Quayle went on: "This Lelley has got some means of getting stuff out of the country. I don't know what it is. I know he's got a contact in Eire. Maybe he's got some other method. He's Himmler trained."

Kerr said: "They're very good." He grinned at Quayle.

Quayle returned the grin. He said: "You ought to know, Ricky."

Kerr said: "So you're a little bored with the Lelley person?"

"Yes," said Quayle. "If you like to put it that way. The point is that I don't propose to send my new agents out—and I want to get them out as quickly as possible—while there's any conceivable chance of Lelley doing anything about it. So—"

Kerr sighed. He said: "So Mr. Lelley is for the high jump?"

"Right," said Quayle. "He's for the high jump."

Kerr nodded. He asked: "When?"

Quayle said: "To-night. I want action."

Kerr said: "I see. Me—and who else?"

Quayle said: "You and Cordover. But listen: I think it's going to be a very good thing if this is an accident. I think it's going to be much easier for all concerned if it's an accident."

Kerr grinned. He said: "You mean the Service Departments won't be annoyed?"

Quayle said: "They can be as annoyed as they like. We come first. My organisation takes the biggest chances and they know it. At the same time the way things are it's going to be a great deal better if this thing is done smoothly."

Kerr smiled. His smile was almost boyish. "That means you've got something really rather nice all worked out?"

Quayle said: "Yes, I've worked it out as far as I can." He brought a piece of paper out of his pocket. He went on: "Look, here's a plan of the house—the Manor House, Nelswood. Lelley's there. At least he was there three hours ago. I've had him under continuous observation for weeks. Now this is how you're going to do it. Cordover will be playing his usual act of driving for that Transport Company. He'll have a truck—a heavy one, but I want to try an experiment before we get down to the real job. You never know, this Lelley might be rather inclined to talk when he realises that things are going to be rather tough for him. He might want to talk a little. He might think there was a chance of saving himself—the usual deal."

Kerr said: "I know—and then if he does talk it doesn't save him?"

Quayle said: "That's right." He drew on his cigarette. "If I ever had any scruples about dealing with this scum crookedly I've lost 'em after the Japanese business. I've got no scruples about Lelley. He's a killer and a sadist."

Kerr said: "I get it. I get in first and offer a deal. If he falls for it and talks—all right. We still go through with the job."

Quayle nodded. "You still go through with it," he said. "And this is how you do it. Come over here, Ricky. Look at this plan . . ."

V

It was cold in the country. The wind came through the open driving window, made Kerr's face tingle. He liked the sensation. Although it had been foggy in London, here it was a beautiful night. There was a moon. In front of the car the road stretched like a white ribbon. As Kerr thought this, he wondered where he had read that crack originally—the one about a road stretching like a white ribbon. He thought the simile was a good one; wondered why the hell he was bothering about what roads looked like anyway.

He took his left hand off the wheel, fumbled in his overcoat pocket for a cigarette. As he did so he could feel beneath his left arm the soft Mexican leather pistol holster. He pressed his arm against it. Kerr liked the feel of the automatic under his armpit. He began to think about automatics.

He had used all sorts and conditions—from a Naval Webley-Scott that would take the top of a man's head off at ten yards, to a little tiny .22 where you either hit them in the pump or you didn't do any harm at all—well, not much. The gun he had with him now was his favourite—a regulation German Infantry Mauser ten-shot automatic firing a cartridge that was as near a .38 as damn. That made a nasty wound. Kerr thought they were good guns. They never jammed. The only thing that happened was sometimes the ejected cartridge case came back and hit you in the middle of the forehead. That, thought Kerr, didn't matter a bit. It told you that the case *had* been ejected. What did matter was what happened to the boyo who got the bullet.

Kerr put the cigarette in his mouth, found his lighter, lit the cigarette. He drew the smoke down deeply into his lungs. The process made him feel just a little sick. Inhaling on too much liquor wasn't so good, he thought. He told himself, as he'd told himself a dozen times during the last six months, that he'd got to ease up a little on this drinking business. One drank too much so easily and it wasn't clever.

He put his foot down on the accelerator; watched the speedometer needle go up to forty-five. He began to think of some of the jobs he'd done for Quayle. . . .

As he went over the crest of the hill he slowed down. Away to the left in the valley he could see the patch of woodland. In five minutes he was on the edge of it. He stopped the car, got out, looked up and down the deserted road. There was no one in sight. He walked away from the car and found, thirty yards away, the gate into the field with the high hedge that Quayle had told him about.

Kerr opened the gate, went back to the car, drove it carefully through into the field, ran it into a nearby thicket. He knew just where to look for the thicket. Quayle had told him that too. As he switched off the lights Kerr thought that Quayle left damn little to chance. He made things as easy as he could.

As easy as he could. But even he couldn't make it too easy. Walking away from the thicket, back towards the gate, Kerr wondered if it were becoming just a little difficult. He wondered if . . . He began to grin. He was grinning at himself—at the idea of Ricky Kerr losing his nerve.

But you *could* lose your nerve, couldn't you? Even first-class fighter pilots had to have a rest sometimes, and he, Kerr, had had damned little rest during the last year. What was the result? You did too much; you took too many chances. So you began to drink a little too much—a sort of natural compensation. The liquor made you confident.

He was at the gate. He realised suddenly that he felt cold. He walked quickly back to the car, opened the cubby hole by the driver's seat; took out a flask of bourbon. He took a long swig; put the flask in his pocket.

He closed the gate carefully behind him, began to walk up the road. A hundred yards farther on he found the fork; the main road branching away to the right over the hill, the left-hand fork little more than a dirt track. Kerr walked along it. Now he was in the patch of woodland. On each side of him the trees were thick. There was a dank earthy smell about the place. Kerr thought it smelt a little like death.

By now the track had become a mere path. A little farther on Kerr came to a clearing. He turned left. Parked in an almost impossible place, on a slope behind some trees, was a truck. It had no lights on. There was something incongruous about the truck, Kerr thought; qualified the thought that there was something incongruous about everything.

Sammy Cordover got out of the driver's cab, closed the door quietly behind him. He stood leaning against the side of the cab, quite relaxed, looking almost happy. He was wearing a suit of stained dungarees. He wore a cloth cap pulled over one eye. An unlit half-smoked cigarette hung from one side of his mouth.

He said: "Good-evening, Mr. Kerr."

Kerr said: "Hallo, Sammy. How is it?"

"It's all right," said Sammy. "How is it with you? You feeling O.K.?"

Kerr said: "I feel fine. Now, there's nothing we need go into, is there?"

Sammy Cordover put his head on one side. Kerr thought that his face looked owl-like in the moonlight. He thought that Sammy Cordover was rather like an owl sometimes. He was a wise bird.

Sammy said: "I wouldn't like to say that. If you wouldn't mind, Mr. Kerr, I'd like you to take a little walk with me. I don't think we ought to take any chances about this set-up. Another thing, I wish I was using a lighter truck. I ought to have brought a lighter one. This goddam thing's like a motorbus. She's heavy on the wheel, too. The tyre pressure's not right." He spat graphically. "When I get back I'm goin' to kick the backside off that basket who looks after these trucks. What the hell does he think he's doin'?"

Kerr said: "Why do you wish you had a lighter truck?"

"You come with me," said Sammy. "You'll see."

They began to walk through the woods, Sammy Cordover a little in front, walking easily and with assurance, his long arms hanging down by his side. Even now, thought Kerr, he's got that jaunty Cockney walk. He smiled. Nothing—not even the imminence of death—could perturb Sammy.

They came out of the edge of the wood suddenly. A road ran between them and what seemed to be the edge of a quarry. They skirted the edge of the wood. Twenty-five yards away was a side road running into the main quarry road at an angle.

Cordover said: "Have you got it, Mr. Kerr?" He grinned. "I can't afford to make a mistake, can I?"

Kerr grinned back. He said: "You won't make a mistake, Sammy."

"I hope not," said Sammy. "I've had one look over the edge of that bleedin' quarry and I don't like it. I'm tellin' you! Still . . ."

Kerr looked at his watch. He said: "I've got twenty minutes. That gives me time to go back, get my car, get into the village."

Cordover said: "Somebody waitin' for you?"

Kerr nodded. "Stott's there," he said. "He's been tailing the boy friend for days. He'll give me all the dirt."

Cordover said: "O.K. You're going to do a little talking, aren't you? So I'll give you half an hour. In half an hour I'll get the old heap out on this road. I'll have the lights on. If anyone should come along—and that's not likely—I'll be having a little engine trouble."

Kerr said: "You've got a load all right, haven't you?"

Sammy grinned. "I'm carrying metal casings," he said. "I'm delivering them to a place twenty-five miles away to-morrow morning at a munitions factory. I *don't* think! Anyway, that's the story."

Kerr put his hand in his overcoat pocket and brought out the flask. He said: "Have a drink, Sammy?"

Sammy put his hands in his pockets. He said pleasantly: "No thanks, Mr. Kerr. I'm not very fond of spirits except now and then. I go for a glass of beer."

Kerr said: "Perhaps you're right." He took a long swig at the flask.

Out of the corner of his eye he could see Sammy watching him. He thought just for a moment that he saw the expression on his face change. He wondered. He put the flask back in his pocket.

He said: "So long, Sammy. I'll be seeing you."

Sammy said: "O.K., Mr. Kerr. Good luck. You'll pull it off. And don't stick your chin out too much, will you?"

Kerr said: "I won't. You keep yours tucked in too."

He began to walk back through the wood.

The man Stott stood in the shadow of an oak tree on the grass verge between the fork of the roads at the top of Nelswood village. He merged perfectly with his background; his drab overcoat, dark brown soft hat, his face which was blue-veined and ruddy, were a part of the shadows. Stott was always like that. Naturally, subconsciously, he placed himself against a neutral background. He was a man who was not noticed. He stood there leaning against the tree, his hands in his pockets, waiting.

He was always waiting for somebody or something. Now he was waiting for Kerr. Before him the narrow winding road led into the unimportant village High Street. The moonlight crystallised the tops of the squat houses making them look as if they had been garnished with sugar icing. Stott thought the scene looked rather like a Christmas card. He began to think about Christmas.

An odd man, Stott. Years ago he had been a trooper in a cavalry regiment. Then he had worked on commission for a tractor firm; then three years in the Mercantile Marine. Stott had been around. He had seen many things, visited many places, before he began to work for Quayle. He liked working for Quayle. It suited him. Most men would have been irked at the inactivity of waiting, at the long hours spent in all weathers, at the continuous passage through crowded streets on the heels of someone on whom Quayle had "put a tail."

But not Stott. He did not mind these irksome processes because they gave him ample time to think.

He could think about Aloise.

Stott considered it extraordinary that a man of his background, upbringing, should ever have married a woman like Aloise. The idea of marrying a woman with a name like that had never seemed quite normal to Stott. He realised that somehow in her own particular way she had lived up to the name. Most of the time that he spent watching and waiting, although his eyes were always wary, he spent thinking about her.

He thought about their marriage—a business which had lasted for five strange weeks—a marriage which had never been consummated—a marriage which had been ended by a laconic telephone message from a call-box telling him that she was going away with someone else. That was three years ago. He had never seen her, never heard of her, since. He wondered what had happened to her. Of course she had been too beautiful for him. She was a slim creature with sleek hips and lovely legs. The first thing that Stott had noticed about Aloise was her legs. He had always been an admirer of beauty. Vaguely at the back of his mind was a mild hatred that he had never even possessed them.

Leaning against the tree, relaxed, his eyes watching the main road down which the car must eventually come, he wondered why she had ever condescended to marry him. There must have been some reason. There must have been some vague desire, some discontent in her mind, some urge towards *something* that he had, some force—no matter how unimportant—which had driven her to stand with him docilely in the registrar's office.

He moved a little. One shoulder was beginning to ache. He thought possibly that one day, in the process of working for Quayle, being sent somewhere to get information about a place or a person, to do one of the dozen important if minor jobs that he did for Quayle, he might find out something about her—might even meet her.

And if that happened? What would he do? He had never allowed himself to consider that aspect of the business. Perhaps, if he were lucky, the question would be answered, the question which had rankled in his mind for so long. He wanted to know why Aloise had married him.

In the distance he heard the noise of an automobile. He drew back nearer towards the trunk of the tree. When the car came up the village street and he was able to distinguish its lines in the moonlight, he recognised immediately that it was Kerr's. Just for a moment he stepped out on to the road—just long enough for the occupant of the car to see him; then he drew back into the shadows.

The car took the left fork. It passed Stott. It drove a hundred yards, pulled into a narrow turning. Kerr got out and came down the road towards the verge. He crossed the road diagonally opposite from Stott; came into the dark circle that surrounded the oak tree.

He said: "Good-evening, Stott."

Stott did not move. He said: "Good-evening, Mr. Kerr. Everything's all right."

Kerr said: "I'm glad to hear it." He took a cigarette case out of his pocket; offered it to Stott who refused; lit a cigarette for himself. He said: "Well?"

Stott said: "It's like this. Keep straight on for three-quarters of a mile. You'll come to another fork. You take the left fork. Another quarter of a mile brings you to the Manor House. It stands right back from the road. You have to drive through a long lane to get to it. That brings you to a five-barred gate. That's the front entrance. The car drive is on the other side."

Kerr said: "But I use the lane?"

Stott said: "Yes. When you get to the gate carry along a little way on the right. There's a good parking place for the car there. No one ever goes there. No one would ever see it. You can pick it up easily there."

Kerr said: "Yes." His voice was cool, but he was feeling the slight tremor of excitement which he had felt lately on these occasions.

Stott went on casually: "The rest of the job's easy. If you go through the gate you're still a long way from the house. You can get round the side of it. There's a white door at the back. Next to it is a window. The catch is broken—you can get in that way."

Kerr said: "I see."

Stott went on: "When you get through the window you are in a scullery. Opposite you is a door leading into the kitchen. Another door on the right brings you to a passageway that leads right through the house to the hall. Usually at night Lelley's in the study—a sort of library—the third door on the left down the passageway. In case you want to know there's a staircase leading out of the hall up to the first floor."

Kerr said: "I'm not interested in the first floor. Who else is in the house?"

Stott said: "There won't be anybody in the house to-night. There's a woman who comes in every day to clean and do the cooking. She goes at eight o'clock. And there's Lelley's man. He's away. He's over at Arpingdon. I don't know what he's doing, but he took the train to-night and he can't get back till to-morrow morning early—not unless he walks, and he won't do that."

Kerr asked: "What cars are there?"

Stott said: "There are two cars, but one's laid up. He's using one—a twenty-five horse-power Morris. He gets petrol because he does a job for the local council at Arpingdon. He doesn't use the car much. Here's a key to the garage Mr. Quayle had cut."

Kerr said: "Thanks. Do you know anything about him? Does he have any contacts around here?"

Stott shook his head. "No," he said. "He's damned clever. And he never meets anybody either. Nobody goes to the house much. He seems to spend most of his time pottering around the garden growing vegetables or something. He's a deep one, this Lelley."

Kerr said: "You're telling me." There was a pause. Kerr drew on his cigarette, took it out of his mouth, looked at its glowing end. He said: "Anything else?"

Stott said: "I don't think so, Mr. Kerr."

Kerr asked: "How long have you been down here?"

"About five weeks," said Stott.

Kerr said: "It must be a pretty boring job."

Stott shrugged his shoulders. He said: "I don't know, Mr. Kerr. You know, I've got a lot to think about."

Kerr said: "That's lucky for you. Would you like a little drink?"

Stott smiled. For a moment his ruddy face relaxed. He said: "Thanks, Mr. Kerr."

Kerr gave him the flask. After Stott had drunk, Kerr took a swig himself. He was beginning to feel quite well—quite happy.

He said: "Well, Stott, you can scram. How do you get back?"

Stott grinned in the darkness. He said: "I do a seven-mile walk; then Mr. Quayle has arranged for a car for me."

Kerr said: "Good. Well, good-night, Stott. I'll be seeing you some time."

Stott said: "I expect so."

He crossed the road, took one of the by-lanes that led behind the village High Street. He disappeared.

Kerr stood leaning against the tree, finishing his cigarette, wondering what it was that Stott thought about all the time.

Lelley stood—one arm resting on the mantelpiece—looking into the fire. A small radio on a Chinese table gave out a waltz softly. Lelley appreciated the music. It was a German waltz.

He was tall; slim. His face was long, but the brow broad, the eyes wide apart and very blue; the nose and jaw prominent. When you looked at his face you became aware of an odd benignity, due possibly to the fact that the eyes were of a quite *soft* blue with a mild expression.

He wore a dark blue silk dressing-gown with black cuffs and collar. He had an air of elegance. Lelley, like most people who followed his profession, was a strange man. Such a profession has need of men who are strange. To be entirely normal, to do the things that Lelley had done, casually—taking them in one's stride—would be an impossibility. Behind the soft blue eyes, the broad forehead, was the scintillating cruel brain of a fanatic.

A strange man. One who was, in his own way, entirely unselfish. Who imagined that he was entirely unconcerned with the things that might happen to him; who believed that he was concerned only with what he could do; what he could make happen; with his own powers and abilities. Sometimes he wondered vaguely what the end would be like. Believed that he would be as indifferent to death as he thought he was to life. He was curious about this aspect; spent much time considering it—almost as if he were contemplating the fate of some other person. Some person in whom he had merely a mild interest. Some person who was not Lelley.

There had been unpleasant things in his life. It had become necessary on occasion to hurt people—to hurt them cruelly. His reasoning would have been that one did not want to hurt people but it was necessary—necessary for the well-being of certain people and certain things—people and things that mattered. It had become necessary for Lelley to hurt even women grievously, but on such occasions he had shown no pang of remorse. The people who had worked closest to him believed secretly amongst themselves that he got a kick out of the process. But if he was a sadist he took the process of sadism in his stride as being necessary to his existence and his work.

He crossed the room, turned off the radio. He began to think about himself objectively. Lelley realised that he was on the top line; that something must happen. He realised that unless the English were even greater fools than some people thought (and for himself Lelley did not believe they were fools), the Paris arrest of the woman Mavrique, followed by the killing of Duborg and Michaelson, must cause some sort of repercussion.

Somebody must know that the information on which the arrest and the killings had taken place had emanated from England. Possibly, thought Lelley, they knew about *him*, in which case they would eventually do something. They would have to. He wondered exactly what they would do. He wondered if they would adopt the same process, use the same technique, as he himself would have used.

He shrugged his shoulders. He moved away from the radio table, lit a cigarette, went back to the fireplace. He leaned against the mantelpiece, stretched his shoulders backwards and downwards. He thought: If they don't do something fairly soon—within a week or a fortnight—it will be my duty to try and get out. He could do that too. He knew a way to get to Eire, and once you were there, well . . . if you were careful, you were all right.

On the other hand, thought Lelley, if they were going to move, they would probably move quickly, especially if they knew all about him. He wondered how much they knew about him; whether they regarded him as not too important, or whether they knew of the supreme organisation which he had evolved during the previous seven years. He smiled a little. He wondered what their attitude would be if they had known that the treatment of British women and prisoners by the Japanese had been part of one of the Lelley schemes. He shrugged his shoulders again. Such things were of course necessary, more especially when one is dealing with people like the Japanese who think so much of *face* that they consider it an additional victory to humiliate and subjugate helpless women and prisoners.

Not for one moment did he think that those who were behind him, who employed him, who had left so much to his clever and facile brain, had let him down; had allowed him at this moment to be thrown to the wolves. That also was part of the game. If he was a sadist he was quite prepared to invert his sadism against himself. Possibly they might even be glad to be rid of him—those greater and more dominant minds. Possibly he knew too much.

He was tired. He yawned. He threw the half-smoked cigarette into the fire. Then, as he half-turned, he saw the library door open slowly; saw Kerr, the Mauser pistol in his hand, come into the room. Lelley raised his eyebrows. He felt mildly interested. He thought in German—an indulgence he only allowed on very special occasions: Here it is. They're on to you. This is it. This is the end. Shall you still be clever enough?

He put his hands into the side pockets of his dressing-gown. He smiled—almost amiably.

Kerr stood in the doorway. He was quite still. The half-smile on his face, for some reason which Lelley could not determine, made him appear to be very cautious.

Kerr said: "Sit down, Lelley. This is where you get yours."

Lelley shrugged his shoulders. He moved over to the large leather armchair, sat down. His movements were slow but graceful. He said: "I was thinking that it was about time that something happened like this."

Kerr allowed the hand that was holding the automatic pistol to drop, to hang straight down by his side.

"So you're not surprised," he said. "That means you've tied all the ends up. That means you're quite ready to die for the Fuehrer."

Lelley said with a smile: "Why not? Death is not so very unpleasant, you know."

Kerr raised his eyebrows. He said: "Really! That coming from you is rather a joke. You've made it damned unpleasant for some people, haven't you?"

Lelley said in a resigned tone of voice: "Those things were possibly necessary, and in any event I do not think it would do any good for us to argue about them."

Kerr said: "Quite." He fumbled in his left-hand overcoat pocket for a cigarette, put it in his mouth, took out his lighter, lit the cigarette. His eyes did not leave Lelley's face. He was thinking: So this is the great Lelley. Himmler's star artiste. The sadist. His nerve's all right. But he's bluffing. Stalling for time. The boy's going to try something before long. Watch yourself, Ricky.

He said: "Don't let me waste my time, but you know on occasions like this there is sometimes a chance of doing a deal."

Lelley smiled. He said: "Really. I imagine that would be the kind of deal which is done so often in our profession. You mean that if I consent to talk I might be permitted to live?"

Kerr said: "Unfortunately—yes. You probably know that the English have a rooted objection to killing people—even people like yourself—in *cold* blood." He grinned to himself as he considered this delightful fable.

Lelley said: "Do you mean to say that you have a number of our people kept in your prisons—people with whom you have made deals?"

Kerr nodded. He said: "That's right. We're such goddam fools we'll let 'em go after the war. Possibly you'll be amongst them. We'll let you go so that you can start organising something else—maybe getting ready for the next war."

Lelley said: "I don't want to talk. I think I'm a little bored with this conversation. May I suggest that we bring it to an end?"

Kerr thought for a moment. Then he said: "Listen, so far as I'm concerned you can have it just which way you like. I don't like you, Lelley. I know all sorts of things about you. Killing you wouldn't mean anything to me. I've killed quite a few of your friends in my time." He grinned a little. "The question is *how* you get killed."

Lelley said: "Meaning what?"

Kerr said: "You used to have a man working for you; his real name was Schmaltz. He did a lot of work for you in Lisbon until somebody caught up with him."

Lelley nodded. He said: "I know. *You* caught up with him."

Kerr said: "That's right. *I* caught up with him. I didn't like Schmaltz very much, because he always shot people through the stomach. As you know that can be a very painful and prolonged process. Perhaps you'd like to experience it—I don't mind."

Lelley said: "Quite naturally when one has to die one would desire to die quickly."

"All right," said Kerr. "That being so I propose to finish this first half of the business according to my orders. You'd better put a coat on." He smiled. "You're a little beyond me, Lelley," he said. "I think someone with a little more brains will have to deal with you. We'll go and see him."

Lelley said: "So somebody else is going to offer me a deal? My reply will be exactly the same and I have no doubt the eventual result will be exactly the same."

Kerr said: "I wouldn't bet on that. The man you'll see might be a little more tough than even I am. He might find the means of making you talk."

Lelley said: "That's possible. I understand everybody has a breaking point."

Kerr said impatiently: "Now *I'm* becoming bored. Put your hands in front of you and keep them there. Let's go and get your coat. I have a key to your garage. Your ignition key's in your car. You and I are going for a little drive. When I've handed you over, my responsibility is at an end, but it's my business to see that I get you there safely."

Lelley got up. He said: "Very well." He walked across the room to the oaken iron-bound door on the other side of the library.

Kerr, the pistol hanging in his right hand, followed closely on his heels.

Kerr was at ease now. Now that he was at work. Now that the thing was moving; being done. He felt tranquil—almost happy and contented.

He thought: Wouldn't it be damned funny if Sandra could see me now. Or would it? I wonder what she'd say. And she thinks I'm with some woman. . . .

He began to smile. He thought it was quite funny.

The headlights cut a swath of hard light contrasting with the soft bright moonlight that flooded the winding country road. The hedges, high on each side of the car, threw back the light into the road. It seemed almost like daylight. There was something uncanny about the peculiar brightness of the atmosphere, something *macabre* in the soft hum of the motor against the silence of the countryside.

Kerr sat relaxed in the back seat of the car. He sat on the left-hand side of the seat, his left hand in his coat pocket, his right hand holding the Mauser pistol lightly against his knee. In front of him, in the driving seat, handling the wheel with practised hands, sat Lelley. Kerr looked at his shoulders. They were easy against the back of the seat; swaying a little with the movement of the car. Lelley was taking things coolly.

A clever bastard, thought Kerr. Very clever. Well . . . people like Lelley had to be clever—or more—to hold their jobs. They were hand-picked at the start, precision trained, turned out to a pattern as regards mental discipline and then, when that process had been achieved, trained again in opportunism and the use of their own particular brands of intelligence.

And they did not give up. Lelley's type never gave up. They might shoot a line or put on an act, but underneath, all the time, they were still working things out, still trying to find the solution of the moment. Just as, at this time, Lelley was trying to find the solution of the moment.

Kerr wondered just what Lelley would try. He thought, acidly: I'd like to know just what you *are* going to try, you son-of-a-bitch. Because you're going to try something. You've *got* to. You're too clever to get yourself into a jam where somebody might get really tough with you and *make* you talk.

You won't do that. You'll try something—*anything*—first, and I bet I know just how you'll do it.

Lelley said casually: "If I continue to drive along this road, if I keep to this road, we make a sweep round Arpingdon and come back into Nelswood. Is that your idea?"

"No," said Kerr. "It isn't. We'll take the first fork on the left and drive past the quarry. When we come to the next fork past the quarry we fork left again and carry on until we get to Paddenham. We're going to stop at Paddenham."

Lelley said: "So your friends are there? The gentleman who proposes to make the deal with me is at Paddenham?"

"Keep your mouth shut," said Kerr shortly. "Keep your eyes on the road and both hands on the wheel. Try anything funny and you get it through the back of the seat, through the stomach. You can have that any time you want it. But don't talk. Talking bores me at this time of night."

Lelley shrugged his shoulders.

In the small driving mirror Kerr saw the shadow of a smile cross his face.

Lelley said: "As you please."

There was silence.

Kerr picked a cigarette out of his coat pocket, lit it, smoked it with pleasure, inhaling great lungfuls of tobacco smoke. He thought that it was an odd thing how one's pleasure in cigarettes varied with different moods. Sometimes you lit a cigarette and it tasted like hell. Another time—as at this moment—and it was marvellous. Just one of those things.

The road widened; the hedges began to disappear. Presently, the surface of the road became rougher. They came to the fork. Lelley swung the car to the left, accelerated as the road straightened under the headlights.

The car began to sway oddly. Kerr sat upright. He thought: So *that's* working all right.

He said: "Take it easy, Lelley. Slow down a bit. Is anything wrong?"

Lelley said: "The car feels heavy on the wheel. I'm finding steering a little difficult."

"Pull over to the left and stop," said Kerr. "Blast it . . . I believe it's a slow puncture. Is there a spare?"

Lelley nodded. "In the back," he said. He braked the car to a standstill.

Kerr said: "I'm going to get out and take a look. Don't try anything funny, will you, Lelley?"

"No," said Lelley evenly, "I won't. What can I try?"

Kerr opened the door, got out. He stopped at the front near side tyre. He bent down, examined it. There was a slow puncture from a defective valve. The air was coming out very slowly but enough to cause a sway at speed. Kerr had expected that. He had fixed the valve himself. It was a nice job.

He looked down the road. The quarry was fifty yards ahead. The moonlight showed on the white chalk surface of the road.

Kerr said: "I'm going to get the spare out and change the wheel. This tyre's all right really. The air is coming out very slowly, but we may have to drive a bit to-night so I'm taking no chances. Just sit where you are, Lelley, and don't move. Keep your hands on the wheel. I shall be watching you all the time, remember."

Lelley said softly: "I shall remember."

Kerr went to the back of the car. He stood a few paces behind the car looking down at the spare wheel compartment. His hands were in his overcoat pockets. The automatic pistol sagged in his right-hand pocket. He stood, biting his lip. He thought: Well . . . this is where you try it. You've *got* to. Come on—get it over.

Suddenly, with a jerk, Lelley started the car. It shot away down the road. It gathered speed. Kerr stood looking at the rear light, grinning. He had thought Lelley would try that one. It was the obvious thing to do. It was the only thing to do. . . .

Kerr stood quite still. He visualised Lelley sitting at the driving wheel, his foot pressed down on the accelerator, thinking that he *still* might get away with it, smiling—that slow benign smile. . . .

Now the ear had accelerated to something near forty miles an hour. Now it was immediately opposite the first bay of the quarry. Inside his coat pockets Kerr's hands were sweating a little. He said softly: "Good luck, Sammy . . . good luck!"

The truck came out of the side road. It came out diagonally on to the quarry road at a good thirty miles an hour. It smashed into the side of Lelley's car; then, as Cordover accelerated and swung the lorry, first towards and then away from the quarry, Kerr could hear the screeching of the tyres of both vehicles as they dragged, at an angle, on the rough surface of the road.

Now Lelley's car was swinging away from the truck. It was bouncing over the road, the rear-end swinging round, towards the quarry's edge. In the split second that followed Kerr saw the off-side door open. Lelley had managed to do that. Then, almost slowly, rear-end first, the car went over the edge.

Kerr stood listening. It seemed a long time before he heard the crash. He began to run down the road towards the truck . . .

Sammy Cordover was standing on the near side of the bonnet. He was wiping his hands on a handful of cotton waste. The dead, half-smoked, cigarette still hung from his lower lip.

He said: "Hallo, Mr. Kerr. That was a bloody near thing, hey? I thought I was goin' over too. I told you I oughta had a lighter truck. An' I know the tyre pressures were all to hell. I'm goddam annoyed about that . . ."

Kerr said nothing. He leaned against the side of the truck. Sammy Cordover went away. Kerr stood there smoking, sucking the smoke down into his lungs, expelling it quickly. He was sweating a little.

Sammy Cordover came back. He said coolly: "Jesus . . . it's not quite so good. Come an' have a look. I don't like it a bit!"

Kerr said irritably: "For Christ's sake . . . what is it?" He went after Cordover.

Standing at the edge of the quarry, looking down in the moonlight, he saw, caught on a spur fifty feet from the top, Lelley's body. It hung grotesquely across the small jutting piece of rock that was just big enough to hold it.

Sammy said slowly: "He got the door open . . . see . . . So he went out first an' the car went after 'im. He fell on that bit stickin' out an' the bleedin' car missed him. It's not so good."

Kerr asked why.

"Supposin' the basket ain't dead?" asked Sammy Cordover. "Supposin' he ain't. . . see? That ain't so good. I got to fix this. You keep an eye on the road."

Kerr nodded. He was feeling just a little cold in the stomach. Not much. Just a little. He moved away from the truck and looked up and down the road.

Sammy Cordover turned out the truck headlights. He left the parking lights on. He went to the back of the truck, got inside, emerged with a coiled manilla rope. He tied the rope round the body of the lorry, threw the end over the quarry. He stood on the edge of the quarry, the cigarette end still stuck on his lip, and looked over. He kneeled down, took the rope in his hands, went over the edge.

Kerr thought: This is a hell of a game . . . Christ, this is a *hell* of a game. He thought quickly. He had his story ready in case—although this was unlikely—someone should appear on the lonely road.

He heard an odd thud. A peculiar soft thud. After a minute or two Sammy Cordover's head appeared over the edge of the quarry. He pulled himself up, picked up the rope, gathered it in, untied the end round the truck, coiled the rope, threw it into the back of the truck. He came towards Kerr rubbing his hands on the seat of his dungarees.

He said: "It's O.K. I pushed him off. An' that's that."

Kerr said: "Was he dead?"

"I wouldn't know," said Cordover. "But if he wasn't, he is now."

"All right," said Kerr. "You stay here, Sammy. You know the story. I'll call the police from Nelswood. Play it as arranged. And don't forget to be suffering from shock. If you can cry a bit it would help."

Sammy Cordover said: "O.K., Mr. Kerr." He was grinning. He went on: "When I thought I was goin' over too I was sufferin' from shock all right. Any'ow one thing was lucky. It was lucky I had the rope. . . ."

Kerr said: "You're telling me."

He was turning away when Cordover said: "If you wouldn't mind, Mr. Kerr, before you go, I'd like that swig of liquor. This night air ain't good for my chest."

Kerr handed over the flask; waited for it to be returned. Then he began to walk quickly towards the woodland, towards the short cut back to Nelswood.

Just behind Nelswood Station, at the end of the dirt road, was the telephone call-box that had been marked on Quayle's plan. Kerr cut his engine, drew in by the side of the road. He got out of the car, went into the call-box.

He switched on his electric torch, found the number. He dialled and stood waiting, leaning against the side of the box. He was wondering whether Lelley had been dead when Sammy Cordover had pushed him off the spur on the quarry-side. Not that it mattered. . . .

The ringing tone went on for a long time at the other end of the line. Two minutes went by and then a gruff voice answered.

Kerr said: "Is that the Police Constable's cottage at Fitchley?"

The voice said it was.

Kerr's voice became tense and concerned. He said: "There's been a terrible accident at the quarry outside Nelswood. A car was driving along the quarry road and a truck came out of the side turning near the Brent fork. The truck smashed into the car and sent it over the edge of the quarry. There was a man inside."

The constable said, almost cheerfully: "That's not very good, is it, sir? I'll get out there at once. Can I have your name? Were you there when it happened?"

"Yes," said Kerr. "I was driving the other way towards Nelswood. I saw the whole thing. Really, it was nobody's fault. My name's Ricardo Kerr. I'm an official of the Ministry of Supply. The name of the driver of the truck—he's standing by there now—is, I understand, Samuel Cordover. He was driving a truck for Meakin and Phelps. Carrying iron castings, I believe. He's pretty badly shocked, I think."

The constable said: "I'm not surprised."

"I'm on important business at the moment," said Kerr. "Business of national importance. So I suggest—as I know you'll want a statement from me—that I call in at the Police Station at Arpingdon and give them such information as I have. I can get there in about an hour—after I've completed my business."

The constable said: "All right, sir . . . thank you. That'll be A1. I'll telephone through to Arpingdon for the police ambulance and I'll get out there right away."

Kerr said good-night. He hung up. He went back to the car, got inside, lit a cigarette. He took the flask out of his pocket and drained it. It tasted very good. He sat there for a little while thinking about Lelley and Cordover and Quayle and himself. Then he started the motor. He began to drive away from Nelswood towards Arpingdon.

Kerr drove along the Fulham Road towards Knightsbridge. It was five-thirty. The streets were very dark. The moon had gone in. He felt cold. He stopped the car at the call-box opposite the hospital. He went into the box, dialled a number.

Very quickly, Quayle's voice said: "Well?"

Kerr said: "This is Ricky. I rang you up because I had a terrible experience when I was out at Nelswood on that Ministry of Supply business a few hours ago."

Quayle's voice was interested. He said: "Really? What happened?"

"A fearful smash," said Kerr. "I was driving past the quarry just outside Nelswood and a car was coming along towards me. A heavy truck drove out of a side turning and knocked the car and the man inside over the quarry edge."

Quayle said: "Not so good."

"Not at all good," said Kerr. "The car was smashed to pieces. I've never seen such a job."

Quayle said: "Well, that's how it goes. What are you going to do now, Ricky?"

Kerr said: "Strangely enough I don't feel awfully tired. Anyhow, I don't propose to go home to-night. I think I'll stay at my usual place—the St. Ermyn's in Knightsbridge."

Quayle said: "All right. Get some sleep. You might look in and see me at the usual place to-morrow about six o'clock. I want to talk to you."

Kerr said: "All right. I'll be there." He hung up.

He got into the car, drove to the St. Ermyn's Hotel in Knightsbridge—a small old-fashioned hotel. They knew him well there. He put the car in the garage, took out from the boot the suitcase that was already packed with clean linen and a change of clothes, went into the hotel.

He said to the ancient night-porter: "Good-morning, Charles. I've had a hell of a journey. I'm very tired."

Charles said: "That means you'd like to sleep to-morrow, Mr. Kerr."

Kerr said: "Yes, I think about lunchtime. I'll have some coffee at one o'clock. I suppose you wouldn't have some whisky in the hotel—not in these days?"

The night-porter said: "Believe it or not, Mr. Kerr, we've always got a little whisky for people we know. I'll bring some up to your room."

Kerr said: "Do that. Make it half a bottle if you can. I shall need a drink in the morning."

VI

Kerr awoke. He lay for a few moments in the transitional stage between sleep and complete awakening. Then, almost in a panic, he remembered his appointment with Quayle. He looked at his wrist-watch. It was five o'clock. He breathed a sigh of relief; put his head back on the pillow.

Outside he could hear the noise of traffic in Knightsbridge. The afternoon light was fading. It would be dark soon.

Kerr began to think about dark streets he had known. The Rua Esteranza in Lisbon—where Fenney had been cut to ribbons and thrown into the gutter. They had found him in the morning with his head nearly severed from his body. There was the Place des Roses—that murky *cul-de-sac* where Fours had his wine shop. There were many dark streets that came to Kerr's mind.

"*There are no shadows in a dark street.*" Confucius or somebody had said that. Well . . . Confucius had a lot to learn. Kerr knew dark streets where there had been shadows—even if you could not see them. Shadows that worked expertly with a garrotter's cord, a knife, a pistol or merely a pair of heavy boots—you could kill a man with a couple of well-placed kicks very nearly as quickly as you could stab or shoot him.

He remembered the "jobs" in Lisbon in the early days of the war—the days when things had been really serious; when you had to move quickly. He remembered the night when he, Kane and Ernie Guelvada, had accounted for eleven enemy agents—most of it done out of doors, most of it done in the dark streets and alleys. He remembered the night when Guelvada had killed Schiltzner by cutting his throat in a mews in Estoril. Guelvada, who was a dead pistol shot, had killed the German agent with a knife because, as he said, "he wanted a nice change."

Kerr began to think about Sandra. He supposed that after he'd seen Quayle he would go home. He would go home and he would find her there. She would be looking quite lovely;

perfectly dressed, and she would look at him sideways out of her lovely violet eyes. She would smile tenderly. There would be no accusation in her eyes, only a vague curiosity.

She would look at him almost as if she were saying: "I wonder what she's like, this woman you've been with. I wonder what attraction she has for you that I haven't got. I wonder what she has to give you that I can't give you." She would say, with just the tiniest hint of sarcasm in her soft voice: "Did they work you very hard at the Ministry, Ricky?" And he would shrug his shoulders.

He would say: "Well, Sandra, you know how it is. There's a war on! There are all sorts of things that have to be done. You can't keep normal working hours in war-time."

She would say: "I know. Have a drink, Ricky."

Probably, thought Kerr, she would be wearing that red frock, a long clinging dress that she wore in the house, a very sophisticated thing. Probably she would be wearing that, with a ribbon in her hair, and she would give him a drink, and he would stand there in front of the fire drinking it, looking at her over the top of the glass, and there would be that thing floating in the air between them.

What the hell! Well, what did you do about a thing like that? What did you *do* about it? Did you turn round and say: "Listen, my dear, don't get me wrong. I wasn't with a woman last night. Oh, I know I'm pretty bad about women. I know there've been women, but believe it or not I wasn't with a woman last night."

And Sandra would say: "No? Don't tell me about anything you don't want to, Ricky." Probably she'd bring a cigarette to him; would light it for him with her long slender, white, fingers. She would give him another drink. Kerr imagined himself saying:

"No, Sandra, I wasn't with a woman last night. I was killing a man out at Nelswood. I'll tell you what we did. When this fellow, who was a German—a most awful bastard—was driving a car along a road by a quarry, Sammy Cordover—that odd little fellow who's been round here to see me once or twice—he's got all the nerve in the world—drove a truck out of a side turning and knocked this chap—car and all—into the quarry. The joke was he got stuck on a spur about fifty feet down. Sammy had to climb down a rope and kick him off. We weren't certain he was dead then, but he's dead now. The quarry is two hundred and seventy feet deep. That's what I was doing last night, my dear. I've done an awful lot of things like that, because . . . maybe somebody's told you there's a war on . . . a war that isn't just fought with aeroplanes and infantry. It isn't only fought on the battle fronts. It's being fought all the time in every city in the world on top and underneath. Well, I'm one of the people who fights underneath."

Kerr visualised himself taking a gulp at his whisky and soda. He heard himself going on, saying: "You remember when I went to Lisbon. I went to Lisbon for the Ministry of Supply, didn't I? That's what I *told* you. Well, I didn't. I met two other men there—a first-class fellow called Kane and a funny little Belgian called Ernie Guelvada. He'd got it in for the Germans because at the beginning of the war some Gestapo tyke cut his girl's breasts off in a captured French village. All right—we had a hell of a time. Somehow or other a whole covey of enemy agents got themselves killed off inside three weeks. That's what I was doing in Lisbon and how do you like that, Sandra?"

Kerr looked at the ceiling. He wondered how she would like it if she knew.

But she would never know. He sat up in bed, stretched. By his side on the bed table was the half-bottle of whisky that Charles, the night-porter, had supplied. Kerr looked at it and raised his eyebrows. There were only three or four inches of whisky in the bottle. He must have had a very good drink the night before, before he went to sleep.

He ran a furred tongue over dry lips. Getting up, getting out of bed, dressing—a difficult process even at this time in the day! He put his hand out for the bottle; finished the whisky. He felt better. He got up; walked towards the bathroom.

It was just six o'clock when Kerr let himself into the house in Pall Mall Place. He went upstairs, found Quayle sitting behind the desk, smoking. He closed the door behind him, stood, looking at Quayle.

He said: "Hallo, Quayle. I'm glad it came off all right."

Quayle said: "Well, Ricky. Come in. Sit down."

Kerr took a chair by the desk.

Quayle said softly: "That's the end of Mr. Lelley. We shan't be troubled with him any more. Everything went very well. Apparently the County police were quite satisfied with Sammy Cordover. They rather sympathised with him in fact. Strangely enough, they'd had that spot—the place where the accident took place—marked as a dangerous place for some time. They've actually been considering closing the side road."

Kerr said: "So everything's all right?"

Quayle nodded. "I spoke to Cordover this morning," he said. "Apparently you had a little trouble with our friend Lelley. He made himself inconvenient up to the last moment."

Kerr said: "You mean falling across that spur in the quarry and having to be pushed off?"

Quayle said: "Yes. It was rather lucky Cordover had the rope." He smiled. "But then Sammy thinks of everything," he said.

Kerr felt in his pocket for his cigarette case. He thought: I wonder what's coming now. I wonder what the next move is. I wonder what he's going to tell me to do now. He realised suddenly that he felt rather tired. When he had lit the cigarette, he looked up and saw that Quayle was smiling at him. He wondered what Quayle was thinking.

Quayle said: "There's a little thing that you can do, Ricky. After that you can have a couple of weeks' leave. Go somewhere and relax. You've done a lot of work during the last two years, haven't you—one way and another?"

Kerr said casually: "I suppose I have. Still—as somebody once told me—there's a war on."

Quayle said: "Yes." He looked away. Kerr realised that Quayle's mind had already jumped to some other thing in some other place; that he was already concerned with some fresh plan.

He said: "What's the little thing?"

Quayle said: "This." He put his hand in his breast pocket, brought out a quarto sheet of paper. There was some typescript on it. He said: "We've got the new agents out in France. They're all settled. To-morrow night Vining will be dropped by plane at a spot behind the Pas de Calais and will take charge of them. Vining's going to be the contact man. He'll go backwards and forwards between here and there keeping touch all the time."

Kerr grinned. He said: "It looks as if you've got a regular passenger service."

"We have," said Quayle. "We're dropping people every night. The thing's rather well organised. We're getting a lot of help from the French." He went on: "Here's a list of the agents, the names that they're known by in France, their locations. Your job is to meet Vining to-morrow morning at Victoria Station. He's catching the eleven o'clock train for Dover. He's got a job to do there and he'll go on from there to the airfield, whence he'll be flown across. You give him this list. He's to learn it off by heart during the train journey. He'll do that quite easily. He's got a mind like a ready reckoner. When he's learned the list off he's to burn it. In other words, the list will be destroyed before he arrives at Dover. I need not tell you that the list is very important."

Kerr said: "You're telling me."

Quayle handed him the sheet of paper. Kerr glanced at the list of names and addresses. He folded it, opened his jacket and his waistcoat, put it in a secret pocket that he'd had made on the inside of his waistcoat.

He said: "Is that all?"

Quayle said: "That's all, Ricky. Meet Vining to-morrow morning. Give him that list. Give him those instructions. Then go off and have a good time."

Kerr said: "That's fine." He got up. "I'm glad the Lelley business went off all right."

Quayle said: "So am I. That fellow was worrying me."

Kerr grinned: "Well . . . he won't worry you any more. Well, so long, Quayle."

"So long, Ricky," said Quayle. "I'll get in touch with you sometime."

Kerr went out. He walked past the St. James's Theatre into St. James' Street up towards Piccadilly. He was feeling better. His mind was at ease. He began to walk along Piccadilly in the direction of Knightsbridge.

Life was a funny business—a hell of a game, he thought. He wondered what Sandra was doing. He wondered what Sammy Cordover was doing.

Thinking about Cordover brought a funny idea into his head. He knew all about Cordover—at least he *thought* he knew. Yet now, at this moment, thinking about Sammy, he had not the remotest idea what he would be doing. What *would* he be doing? Kerr realised that really he knew very little about Sammy; that he knew just that Sammy who accompanied him on jobs; just that person who was so very adequate when nerve was required, when things became a little tough. But outside that . . . ?

Of course, he knew nothing of Sammy. He knew nothing about his private life, his hopes, fears, desires, pastimes, hobbies or women. Nothing at all.

Well . . . soldiers were like that, weren't they? You fought with a man. You lay in a slit trench with him, went over the top with him, killed Germans with him. You thought you knew all about him, but in effect you knew sweet Fanny Adams about him. You probably didn't even know where he lived, what he did, what he thought. Why should you? Your intimacy with him was due to the accident of war, but his private life still belonged to him just as your own life belonged to you.

Kerr went into the bar at the corner of Sloane Street and drank a double whisky and soda. He came out, lit a cigarette, began to walk along Knightsbridge in the direction of the Brompton Road.

He felt oddly elated. A peculiar and not-too-well-understood feeling of well-being possessed him.

He continued to walk. He was contented to walk. He took no particular heed of direction. Once or twice he turned down a side street to the left or right without any particular idea as to what the street was, or whence it led.

He stopped—suddenly. He was in a Square. Kerr stood and looked about him and told himself that it was a nice Square. It had an air. The architecture of the houses was good. The houses had atmosphere. The Square was spacious and, in the middle, were some gardens. He wondered where he was. Vaguely, he seemed to remember the place, but rather as if he had known it in some other city, some other country. He did not remember it as being part of London. Not any part that he knew.

He walked through the Square. On the other side he came into a narrow street, and half-way down the street, on his right, he saw an arched opening. At the bottom of the passageway, forming a *cul-de-sac*, was a public house. It was an old place with leaded windows, and an antique sign swung above a gothic door which formed the entrance. Kerr thought that it looked rather like a church which had been turned into a pub. The idea amused him.

He turned into the *cul-de-sac*, went into the public house. The inside was as amusing—as strange—as the exterior. The saloon bar, in which Kerr found himself, was a long room, "L" shaped and with a low ceiling. At the end was an alcove.

The place was crowded. There was a low hum of voices and a miasma of tobacco smoke hung on the air. Kerr went to the end of the room and sat on a high stool before the bar. He ordered a double whisky and soda.

Suddenly he felt tired—very tired. He thought that when he had drunk the whisky and soda he would go home. He would go home and go to bed. The thing to do was to sleep.

The voices round him rose and fell in a peculiar metre of sound. There seemed a certain rhythm in the hum of conversation. Everyone, thought Kerr, seemed to have an awful lot to say and to be saying it in the most confidential tone of voice. Then a voice stood out.

An American voice said: "Jeez . . . fellers, what a babe!"

Turning, Kerr saw that it was a soldier who had spoken. He turned on his stool and followed the direction of the soldier's gaze. He could not see because the man was looking into the "L" shaped piece of the bar—the piece at the top of the room.

Kerr got off the stool and, glass in hand went to the top of the room and looked. He stood there, looking straight in front of him, with an expression of vague surprise on his face.

He saw the woman.

She was sitting on a high stool, half-leaning against the wall which bounded the end of the bar. She was unutterably lovely. She sat, her hands, gloved, clasped in her lap, looking straight in front of her. She looked like death.

Kerr passed through into the "L" shaped piece of bar and stood uncertainly looking at her. He felt vaguely uncomfortable.

She was quite perfect. She wore a moss-green coat and skirt with astrakhan facings. She wore no hat and her hair was the colour of Indian ink. Her face was dead white. Her eyes looking straight in front of her were blue.

Her shoulders were hunched forward a little. Like that Kerr could see the curve of her hips on the stool, the trim waist, the soft line of the shoulders. Her legs were long and her skirt caught tight against her showed their shape. They were quite lovely. Her feet, perched on the rail of the stool, were small, superbly shod.

Kerr stood looking at her. He said to himself: Christ, Ricky . . . what are you going to do about this? It was obvious to him that something must be done about it. The idea of drinking his drink and going away had become impossible.

He moved forward, sat on the empty stool at her side. He looked at her. She continued to look straight in front of her. She looked quite hopeless, unutterably despairing.

Kerr said: "You ought to cheer up a little. Nothing is quite as bad as it seems. Nothing ever is. Not really. You ought to believe that because it's true." He smiled at her. He was thinking that the sound of his voice sounded a little strange to him.

She turned her head. She looked at him. Kerr saw that she was wearing a pale green chiffon blouse caught at the throat with a diamond and ruby clasp. He thought that her clothes had cost a hell of a lot of money. He wondered what she was doing in this place.

She said in a low and tremulous voice: "It's nice of you to try to cheer me up. Thank you. I'm afraid that it's useless."

Kerr said: "Nothing's useless." He spoke quickly. He was thinking that whatever happened she must be made to talk; that she must not be allowed to go until she had talked. He was obsessed by the proximity of this woman. Now, as she still faced him, he caught a suggestion of the perfume she was wearing.

He went on: "Nothing's useless. Everything means something. Everything will be better to-morrow. Everyone has bad spots occasionally, you know. Life's like that."

She said: "You're very kind. I wish I could agree with you. I wish I could think you were right."

Kerr said: "Please tell me . . . what's the matter? Is there anything I can do?"

She shook her head. She said: "I've been walking about, going into saloons and bars and places and drinking—a thing I've never done before—since early evening. I did that because someone once told me that if you drink a great deal you forget things. But that isn't true. I've forgotten nothing."

Kerr asked: "What are you trying to forget?"

She said very softly: "I had two brothers. I was very fond of them. I loved them dearly. They were both shot down over Germany on the same day—last week. This afternoon I was told that my husband has been killed in Italy. We were married four months ago. Can you understand how I feel? I want to die. It is quite impossible to continue to live. It would not be worth while."

Kerr said: "That's pretty bad. I know how you feel. It's not so good. But what can you do about it?" He put out his hand. He took her small gloved hand in his. He pressed it and laid it back in her lap. The action was sensitive and charming.

She said: "I like you. I think you are very kind. I think you must have suffered a great deal yourself. Thank you."

Kerr beckoned to the barmaid. He ordered two double brandies and sodas. He said:

"You ought to drink rather a lot to-night. And then you should go to bed and sleep. I don't suppose you've slept a great deal lately."

She said: "I haven't slept at all. I don't think I shall ever sleep again."

The girl brought the brandies and soda. Kerr said: "Drink that. You'll feel better."

She drank the brandy. Kerr began to talk to her. His voice was soft and restful. He told her stories, incidents, experiences, all with the point that nothing ever really matters a great deal; that time heals and changes all things; that to-morrow is another day. He talked and talked. There was a certain urgency in the back of his mind, an urgency that prompted him to talk; not to stop talking. He thought that if he stopped talking she might go. He thought he could not bear that.

She sat quite still and listened. Sometimes she looked at him. Once or twice searchingly. When she looked at him Kerr felt odd and peculiarly elated. Once or twice she spoke and Kerr watched the perfect contour of her lovely mouth break and show the white teeth beneath.

Every now and then he ordered more brandy. He felt quite cool; quite sober. He felt that this meeting, coming as it had after the Lelley thing, was right and proper. He felt that somehow it had been ordained.

At ten o'clock she said: "I must go. Will you please take me away. I live on the other side of the Square. If you would please see me to my door . . ."

They went out of the inn. Outside it was bright moonlight. They began to walk across the Square.

She put her arm through Kerr's. The proximity of this woman affected him more than anything else that had ever happened to him, he thought. He wondered what was going to happen about this. If anything was going to happen. He thought something must happen . . . it *must.*

They came to a door and stopped. She said: "Thank you so much. You've been so very kind to me. Good-night."

Kerr said: "This sounds ridiculous but I don't want to leave you. If I do I shall probably never see you again. That would be impossible. . . ."

She said: "I am a very selfish person. It never occurred to me that *you* might be unhappy too. . . ."

Kerr said nothing. Somewhere—a long way away—he could hear the noise of traffic. A hundred miles away.

She said: "Would you like to come in and have a drink? I could give you a drink . . ."

Inside, in the cool hall, there was the scent of flowers. Kerr stood in the darkness. Then a light was switched on. He put down his hat and went into the room.

It was a delightful room. He saw a bookcase and some old furniture and the glow of a fire. The light was dim. He stood there, trying to bring his mind to some sort of coherent reasoning; to understand what he was trying to do.

She brought him the drink. It was in a glass that was fragile and of a peculiar shape.

Kerr took the glass in his left hand. He said, thank you. He looked at her.

She stood in front of him looking at him. Her eyes were tired and unhappy. Her mouth was trembling.

She said: "Do you think . . . do you think . . . ?"

Kerr put out his right arm and took her. He drew her close to him. He crushed her against him. With a supreme sense of elation he felt the soft slimness of her body yield to him.

She put her mouth to his. Kerr could feel the tears streaming down her face.

He crushed the glass in his left hand. He crushed it and heard the pieces tinkle on the polished floor. As she strained closer to him he could feel the warm blood from his cut hand running down his fingers . . .

The sunlight came through the window, made a grotesque shadow on the floor. Kerr, his eyes half-opened, looked for a long time at the shadow, tried to identify it. He lay, his head pillowed on his arm, his eyes dim, looking at the sunlight. He became a little more awake. He saw that the room was papered with red; that the furniture was gold—second Empire furniture. The bed itself was gold and the heavy quilt, half of which was trailed down to the floor, was of red silk. He wondered why he should be in a gold bed with a red silk coverlet.

He yawned, stretched himself. He put his head back on the pillow and remembered . . .

He thought for what seemed to be a long time. He found some peculiar satisfaction in reiterating in his mind the events of the previous evening and night. His left hand hurt a little. He remembered crushing the glass. He remembered everything.

He moved a little in the bed. He thought: This is the next day. This is the time for recrimination, for questions, for wondering why one did this or that. This was one of those things.

He remembered the woman—everything about her—that marvellous strange exotic and quite delightful person. In a few minutes she would probably awake and remember her own miseries. Well, he might be able to help a little there. He might . . .

Kerr took pleasure in visualising what she would look like at this hour of the morning, with the sunlight coming through the window. He turned his head. He saw she was not there.

He became quite awake. He wondered where she was. Was she downstairs possibly wondering why? Or making coffee and not wondering why—or bathing?

Kerr got out of bed. He stood in the sunlight, quite naked. On a chair on the other side of the room was a silk robe—hers. He wrapped it round himself. He went out of the bedroom, downstairs, to look for her.

The house was empty—not only empty, but the rooms, as he went through them, presented to him a peculiar lifelessness. Somehow, in some weird way, the atmosphere of the large, well-furnished rooms seemed to press on Kerr. He wondered where the hell she was. He stood in the middle of the drawing-room, the pale blue silk robe incongruously wrapped round him.

Probably she had gone out. She had awakened. She had found Kerr in her bed. He smiled. Probably the fact had surprised her. Then she had remembered. She'd got up, crawling across him, dragging the red silk coverlet with her. She had dressed and gone out. Probably she wanted to think. Kerr could understand that. That would be the explanation.

He walked towards the stairs. He began to think about Sandra. He stopped suddenly. She had been right after all. *There had been a woman.* Kerr grinned wryly. There hadn't been one really but there was one *now*. He remembered the little scene he had rehearsed with her when he had been lying in bed at the St. Ermyn's Hotel before he had kept his appointment with Quayle. And so much had happened since then.

He began to move up the stairs. He wanted a cigarette. Suddenly an extraordinary feeling possessed Kerr. It was as if icy fingers had been laid on his brain. He moved quickly up the stairs. The silk robe slipped from his shoulders to the floor. He opened the door of the bedroom: then—remembering—he came out of the bedroom, moved across the passageway into the bathroom.

In the corner was the chair on which he had put his clothes the night before. Always tidy, he had hung his waistcoat and coat over the back of the chair. But now the coat lay on the floor and the waistcoat with it.

He moved slowly across the room, picked up the waistcoat, tore open the secret pocket on the inside. The list of Quayle's new agents in France—the list of their names, their addresses, everything about them, which was to be delivered to Vining, was gone!

The hand holding the waistcoat dropped to Kerr's side. He walked slowly back to the bedroom. He sat down on the edge of the bed. The patch of sunlight—the grotesque shadow—was still on the floor.

The waistcoat fell from his fingers. He rested his head in his hands, sat looking blankly at the wall before him.

He said: "Oh . . . my God . . . Oh, my God!"

CHAPTER TWO
QUAYLE—CORDOVER—O'MARA

I

Mrs. Selby—buxom, grey-haired, fifty-five years of age—pushed open the door of Sammy Cordover's bedroom. She stood in the doorway looking at him.

The picture was without beauty. He lay, one leg outside the bedclothes, his head stretched back on the pillow, his mouth wide open, snoring. The noise, Mrs. Selby thought, was rather like that of a buzz-saw.

She shook him by the shoulder. She said: "It's past ten o'clock, Mr. Cordover. Do you want your breakfast now?"

Cordover opened his eyes. He regarded her balefully. She thought he looked very tired. She thought it was a great shame that such a weedy-looking person as Sammy should be forced to drive heavy trucks about the countryside all night. The Ministry of Supply must be hard up for drivers if they had to use people like Sammy Cordover And he was such a nice boy really. He tried sometimes to look tough, but you knew, of course, that he wasn't really. She made a mental comparison between Sammy and her own strapping son who was in a Commando unit—a *real* man. She thought they ought to get a bigger, stronger, man for a job like Sammy's.

Cordover said sleepily: "I'll have a nice pot of tea, Mrs. Selby, an' one piece of toast an' marmalade. Make it snappy."

She went away.

He sat up in bed. At the back of his mind was a remote sensation of pleasure—of something which he could not quite remember, but which pleased him. He looked round the untidy bedroom. He grinned. Propped against the wall on the other side of the room was a large cardboard box; on it the name of a popular firm of tailors. He remembered that he had ordered a new suit; that this would be it.

He got out of bed, went to the mantelpiece, found a cigarette, lit it. He stood looking at the cardboard box wondering about the suit.

It was characteristic of Sammy Cordover that the events of two nights before had left no mark on his mind. He remembered them in exactly the same way as a green-grocer might remember selling a cabbage to a special customer. That was all. The business of having a new suit was much more important. Very often Sammy had been concerned in affairs akin to that one which had happened at the Nelswood quarry. He was inured to them. His nerves, attuned to excitement and danger, stretched and contracted easily. Such things was his job.

He undid the string about the box, took out the suit. He hung it carefully over the back of a chair, put on an old woollen dressing-gown, sat down and waited for Mrs. Selby.

His breakfast finished, he wondered what he should do with the day. He began to think about Quayle. Quayle would not want him for a bit. Sammy knew enough about the technique of the game. He knew that when you had done a job like the Nelswood one you got four or five weeks off and if anything happened in the meantime somebody else had to handle it.

Somebody else . . . Sammy wondered just how many other people were doing the same sort of job as he did, as Ricky Kerr did; just how many other people had secret and mysterious appointments with people like Lelley who disappeared suddenly in one way or another; just how many people Quayle had on his books. There was a strange bloke, thought Sammy. A fly one, that one—one who never let his left hand know what his right hand was doing. You knew just enough and that was all. Deep inside him, Sammy had an admiration almost amounting to affection for his employer. He sensed the responsibilities that lay heavily on Quayle's shoulders.

But you felt safe with Quayle. When he put you into a job everything was ready-eyed—everything was planned. Of course there could be a slip-up. Sammy Cordover remembered two or three occasions when it had been a narrow thing; when something had gone wrong. But that was one of the chances you took. Anyway, you got dam' well paid for it. And you even got a few extra coupons sometimes—enough to get yourself a new suit.

He began to shave and dress. When he had finished he found a little difficulty in seeing the entire effect of the new suit. It was blue and ultra smart with the usual double-breasted, high-waisted, effect which Sammy admired so much, with rather wide knife-creased trousers falling over shoes that were a little pointed. Unfortunately, the mirror set on the dressing-table enabled you to see only half of yourself at a time. Still, even that way he was pleased.

The telephone rang noisily. Sammy jerked his head in the direction of the instrument. He thought: That's dam' funny. It flashed through his mind that never before had the telephone rung so soon after a job had been completed. Only two people used Sammy's telephone number, and they were the girl in Quayle's office and Quayle himself. He wondered what had happened.

He took off the receiver. It was the girl in Quayle's office. Cordover had never seen her but he liked her voice.

She said: "Mr. Cordover, Mr. Quayle wants to speak to you."

He said: "O.K." He waited.

Quayle said: "There's a Lyons tea-shop just off Ryder Street in St. James', Sammy, with a self-service counter downstairs. Can you be there in twenty minutes' time?"

"O.K., Mr. Quayle," said Sammy. He thought: Well, what do you know about that? What the hell's poppin' now?

He stood in the middle of the bedroom, drawing on the cigarette stub, wondering. Never before had Quayle got on to him so soon after a job. Well, maybe something had happened. Maybe something had gone wrong. He shrugged his shoulders.

He took the dark blue soft hat of American shape from its hook behind the door, set it on his head at a jaunty angle. He went out.

Quayle was sitting at a marble-topped table, drinking coffee. Cordover went to the service counter, got a cup of coffee, paid for it. He walked over, sat down beside Quayle.

He said: "Good-morning, Mr. Quayle. Anything wrong?"

Quayle smiled. His smile was almost reassuring.

He asked: "Why, Sammy?"

Cordover grinned. "The only time you ever ring me up is when you want me to do something—you or that young lady of yours. I've never been rung up before after a job. I wondered if something had slipped up—something had gone wrong."

Quayle said almost casually: "A lot's gone wrong, Sammy."

Cordover said nothing. He thought: I wonder what he's going to put on my plate now. Maybe it's going to be tough. I wonder who's slipped up.

Quayle went on: "I don't often let you into my confidence. I don't think it's a good thing to do, Sammy. I think it's much fairer to the people who work for me to let them know just as much as they ought to know and no more."

Cordover said: "It's a good idea, Mr. Quayle. If somebody gets hold of 'em they can't talk because they don't know."

Quayle smiled. "Right, Sammy," he said. "However, I'm going to talk to you now because I've got to. We're in a little bit of a jam."

Sammy sunk his voice. "Anything to do with the job of the night before last," he said, "that Lelley guy?"

Quayle said: "Yes . . . and no. The thing is that Mr. Kerr was given a list of people working for us in occupied France. That list was to be handed over this morning at eleven o'clock to an operative of mine who will be dropped from an aeroplane in France to-night. You understand that that was a very important list?"

"You're tellin' me," said Sammy.

Quayle went on: "Last evening, Mr. Kerr, who had the list in an inner pocket in his waistcoat, went to a pub called the Green Headdress. He met a woman there." Quayle grinned wryly. "Apparently a very attractive woman. They got into conversation. It seems that she had had a great deal of trouble lately. Two brothers had been shot down over Germany in one day and then she'd lost her husband."

Cordover said: "Blimey! She has been havin' a rough time, hasn't she?"

"Yes," agreed Quayle. His voice was sardonic. "She and Mr. Kerr had a few drinks together and he went to her home. He stayed there the night. This morning he found himself alone in the place, and the list was gone."

Sammy Cordover said: "Jesus . . . !"

Quayle nodded. "I agree with you," he said.

There was a silence; then Cordover asked: "What do you want me to do, Mr. Quayle?"

Quayle said: "Sammy, you've worked a great deal with Mr. Kerr. I think you two have done about sixteen or seventeen jobs together. You know him pretty well, don't you—and you like him?"

Cordover nodded. He said: "Yes, I like him a lot. He's a nice bloke—attractive. I've often watched him walkin' down the street; wished I was like him."

Quayle asked: "You admire him merely for his appearance?"

Cordover said: "No, he's quick, you know, an' clever, and he can be very tough. At least . . ."

Quayle said quickly: "What do you mean by 'at least,' Sammy? Remember, won't you, that what we're saying now is important. Remember that people's lives depend on it."

Cordover said: "You mean that list?"

Quayle said: "I mean that list."

There was another pause. Sammy Cordover drank a little coffee, produced a packet of cigarettes, lit one. He said:

"You know, Mr. Quayle, I've once or twice lately thought perhaps Mr. Kerr was slippin' a bit, if you know what I mean. He likes a drink. I've noticed that. I thought he'd been drinking a bit too much lately. I thought maybe he was gettin' a bit tired."

Quayle said: "Anything else?"

Sammy said: "Well, I don't know. You see things, and you get ideas, but they're not always right. Once or twice when I've been round at his place I've noticed Mrs. Kerr sort of lookin' at him sideways—you know, sort of curious. Once or twice I got around to wonderin' what was on her mind—that is if there *was* something on her mind."

Quayle said: "What do you think is the sort of thing that would be on the mind of a woman like Mrs. Kerr?"

Sammy rubbed his chin with a finger. He said: "*I* wouldn't know. But you know, Mr. Quayle, Mr. Kerr is a guy that women would go for in a very big way. He used to go to a lot of parties. He knows some very swell-looking women. I've seen him with them."

Quayle said. "Ah!"

Cordover went on: "You know, Mr. Quayle, perhaps you wouldn't mind if I said something to you—something that you might think was a bit out of turn?"

Quayle said: "You say anything you like."

Cordover looked at the table. He said: "You know, Mr. Quayle, Mr. Kerr's rather like a racehorse, isn't he—sort of drawn out. D'you know? If he's going to do something he puts everything he's got into it. I was watchin' him the other night when we was doing this job at Nelswood. He was on edge—right on his toes. He's always been like that when it comes to the time; like they say about an actor who's just going on the stage—sort of stage fright. O.K. When the job's over—when it's done—he's inclined to flop a bit, see? He had a few drinks. That's why I'm a bit surprised, Mr. Quayle."

Quayle asked: "Surprised at what?"

Cordover said: "You're no, mug, Mr. Quayle. You're all brains. I should think you're the cleverest man in this country. I haven't worked for you for as long as I have without know-ing what you have to do—what you're up against. That's why I can't understand that you don't know that about Mr. Kerr; that sort of flopping for a bit when the job's done. I shoulda thought you'd have noticed it."

Quayle said: "Well, supposing I had noticed it?"

Cordover looked at him. He said: "Well, Mr. Quayle. He got that list. He had to deliver it directly after he'd done the other job. That's what surprises me."

Quayle said: "It's a good point, Sammy, but after all, you know, a job's a job. It's all very well to talk about reactions and flopping after a job—"

Sammy said: "I know, Mr. Quayle. I know. . . ." He waited.

Quayle said: "I saw Mr. Kerr this morning. He came to me. He told me the story. He went back to the Green Headdress. They'd never seen that woman before. It's an extraordinary coincidence that she should have been in that bar when he went in—because, remember, he'd never been there before; that she would be the one person who wanted that list."

Cordover said quickly: "Was he certain she was there when he got there?"

Quayle grinned. He said: "I thought you'd get on to that, Sammy. Of course she wasn't there when he got there. She came in after him."

Cordover said: "My God . . . so they had a tail on him. He was followed. That means—"

Quayle said grimly: "Exactly. That means that somebody was on to Kerr. That means he was picked up either coming back from the Lelley job or that they kept after him all the time; that that woman went in after him; that they knew sufficiently about him to know how he reacts when he's had a few drinks."

Sammy said: "You mean they might have been wise to the Lelley business?"

Quayle shrugged his shoulders. "Why not?" he said. "You know, we're not the only people in this game. The Germans have got some first-class people too. Lelley was one of them."

Cordover said quickly: "Listen, Mr. Quayle, you had a reason for going out for Lelley. You wanted him bumped, didn't you? I don't know why."

Quayle said: "I *had* to have him bumped as you call it, Sammy. Lelley was the person who was getting information out of this country about our agents in France. We lost three of them not long ago—traceable directly to him. He had to go."

Cordover said: "Look, Mr. Quayle, isn't it on the cards that they knew you'd be on to Lelley; that somebody would be on to Lelley; that you'd know that it was him who gave those people away?"

Quayle nodded. There was a little gleam of admiration in his eyes. He said: "I think you're right, Sammy. I know what you're going to say. You're going to suggest that the people who employed Lelley knew we'd get after him. They knew we'd traced it to him. They knew we'd get him just as they would have done if they'd been in our position. So they kept Lelley under observation. They waited for us to do something about him."

Cordover said: "That might be true, but even if they'd been hanging around there in Nelswood, they couldn't have tailed Mr. Kerr back. They couldn't have taken a chance like that. There are no cars on the road at nights. He'd have seen that they were tailin' him."

"Right," said Quayle. "So there was somebody who could give them an indication—somebody who could give them an indication that he was going down to Nelswood; somebody who knew what his job was, and somebody who could guess the night it was going to come off. Now, what does that make you think, Sammy?"

Sammy said: "Well . . ." He paused for a moment. Then: "I didn't know anything about it until you phoned me through, Mr. Quayle. And I got through to him at that party—the party at Mrs. Milton's house. *Jeez* . . . !" He stopped suddenly.

"Right," said Quayle. "Somebody at that party knew that Lelley was for the high jump. Somebody at that party knew Kerr was working for me; somebody at that party was able somehow to pick up Kerr when he came into London. That would be easy enough; there's only one way he'd come back. They were on to him from the moment he arrived."

Sammy said: "They'd be on to him when he came round to see you the day after. Where did he see you, Mr. Quayle? They'll be on to that place." His voice was urgent.

"That's all right, Sammy," said Quayle easily. "I've closed it down. We shan't use it any more."

Cordover drew on his cigarette. He said: "It's not so good, is it, Mr. Quayle? It's not so good." He went on: "Look, Mr. Quayle, I think you're a bit worried." His voice became diffident, his expression almost a little ashamed. He said: "You know I'd do anything for you; anything for Mr. Kerr—and Mrs. Kerr."

Quayle said softly: "You *like* Mrs. Kerr, don't you, Sammy?"

Sammy said: "Like her? She's like a bleedin' goddess to me. She's the most lovely thing I've ever seen in my life, Mr. Quayle. I could just stand and look at her." An idea came to him. He frowned. He said: "Look, does she know anything about what Mr. Kerr does; about his working for you?"

Quayle shook his head. "Not a thing," he said. "She thinks he works for the Ministry of Supply."

Sammy nodded. He said: "What do you want me to do, Mr. Quayle? You tell me and I'll do it."

Quayle said: "Listen, Sammy. That woman's got that list."

Cordover said: "Yes, and there's another thing, Mr. Quayle. If she's got that list, what about the bloke who's going over to France; who's going to be dropped to-night? It's not so good for him, is it? What are you going to do about that?"

Quayle shrugged his shoulders. "I can't do anything about it," he said. "I have had a duplicate list sent down to him. My only hope is that by the time he arrives and begins to make use of that list, we can do something over here. If not . . ."

Cordover said: "If not, they'll be on to all our people in France. God help 'em."

Quayle said: "That's right, Sammy."

Cordover thought for a moment; then: "Well, all right, Mr. Quayle, so this woman's got the list. She's got to pass it to somebody, hasn't she? What are they going to do about it?"

"Normally," said Quayle, "if they wanted to get it out of this country quickly, if they wanted to get it over the other side, they'd have done it through Lelley, wouldn't they? Well, they can't do it through Lelley. Lelley's dead. So there's somebody else; someone we don't know about."

Cordover said: "That's sticking out a foot."

"All right," said Quayle. "We've got to find them somehow. I think that there's a connection between this business and the party at Mrs. Glynda Milton's. Well, we've got to move quickly. If necessary, we've got to be very tough. Now listen to me, Sammy. . . ." He bent his head closer over the table.

II

Kerr walked along Piccadilly. It was nearly noon; the streets crowded with the war-time collection of humanity that concentrates at midday in that area. Kerr did not see the people even if he appeared to be looking at them. His mind was in a peculiar state which even he did not understand. There was something worse than remorse in it. He felt rather like a man whose duty it is to sentence himself to death.

He remembered his interview of an hour or two ago with Quayle. Kerr had wondered before the interview just what Quayle's attitude would be. He had been scared because he was aware of the complete and utter ruthlessness that existed in Quayle. He had been surprised. Quayle had accepted his fearful story almost as if he were not surprised by it. He had said only one thing.

He had said, almost casually: "Of course this is a little bit tough on Vining and the people over in France. I can't stop Vining going. He's got to go this morning. He must be in France to-night. All I can do is to send him down a duplicate of the list I gave you and hope that somehow your lady friend won't be able to get *her* list to her friends too quickly. If she does it's not going to be so good for our people, is it? You know what the Germans will do with them, don't you, Ricky?"

Kerr turned into Berkeley Street. Now, as he approached his home, he began to think of Sandra. He thought bitterly that in the normal course of events he would have put up some story for her benefit—a story to explain his absence. Now he felt that he wanted to explain nothing. He was filled with a peculiar self-loathing; was disinclined to talk to anybody. He wished he could stop thinking.

Quayle had said: "You'd better take a few weeks' leave, Ricky. Then I'll find you another job."

Kerr had said: "That's pretty decent of you, Quayle. I thought after this I should have been laid off. I should not have liked that."

Quayle had looked at him and said: "Oh, you'll get another chance some time. They say that experience teaches us. Maybe this business will teach you something. But—" he smiled at Kerr; had gone on: "you won't slip-up again. Anyhow, if you did, it wouldn't be awfully good for you. I promise you that, Ricky."

The sun came out. The day was cold but pleasant. Berkeley Street was filled with pretty women. One of them laughed suddenly—a pretty tinkling sort of laugh. Kerr felt that he hated the sound. He felt that he'd like to strangle the woman for being able to laugh like that.

He crossed Berkeley Street, got out of the lift on the third floor at his apartment block, walked down the corridor, opened the door, went into his flat. Invariably when he arrived home, he experienced a peculiar sense of well-being, due probably to the charming decoration of the flat, its friendly atmosphere and the delightful feminine touches provided by the expert fingers of Sandra.

Kerr hung up his things; went into the drawing-room. It was empty. He wandered through the flat looking for Sandra.

Apparently she had gone out. He called her but there was no reply. He wandered slowly into her bedroom; saw propped against the mirror on her dressing-table a square envelope. Written on the front were the words *For Ricky.* Often she left notes for him there. This one probably said where she had gone—when she would be back.

Kerr stood with the envelope in his fingers looking out of the window. After a moment he opened the envelope, read the note. It said:

"Dear Ricky,

"This is probably going to give you a shock. But I don't think that a shock is going to be very bad for you and in any event I don't see how I can hurt you very much.

"Of course, men being what they are, your pride will be hurt. But then, my dear Ricky, my pride's been hurt a great deal too, lately, so perhaps we can cry quits on that.

"I am going to leave you—not because I'm bored or unhappy (although quite candidly I have been bored and unhappy for the last three or four months); not because of your strange absences from home, explained almost casually as if they didn't matter, and sometimes so badly that I believe you weren't even trying to find a good lie. I'm going because, believe it or not, I've fallen very deeply in love. He's not your sort of person, but I love him, and I don't think I mean suffi- cient to you for you to worry about the fact of my leaving you.

"I don't know what you'll want to do about this, but I expect in your own time, when you've thought about it, you'll let me know.

"Don't treat this lightly or casually, or think that it's just one of those things (I can almost hear you saying to yourself as you read this, that this is just one of those things) because it isn't. Don't make any mistake about that.

"Bless you, Ricky. We've had some marvellous times together. It's a great pity things have to be like they are, isn't it?

"Sandra."

"P.S.—By the way, you ought to know, of course—the man is Miguales."

Kerr folded the note, put it in his jacket pocket. He walked slowly to the dining-room. He poured out a large whisky and soda. He stood leaning against the cocktail cabinet looking vaguely at the wall opposite. He said to himself: It never rains but it pours. They say things come in threes. Well, if they're right, I wonder what the *third* thing is going to be. By God, I'd like to know . . . because if it's going to be tougher than the other two it's not going to be so goddam good!

Meet Shaun Aloysius O'Mara. If a little time is taken in the presentation of Mr. O'Mara it is because the picture is worth while.

He was tall and very big. He reminded one of a bull, except that, when you looked at his face, you were conquered immediately by a deep and peculiar charm which can only live in a certain type of Irishman.

Mr. O'Mara believed that the world was a very good place. Quite obviously, at any moment of the night or day, he was satisfied with it. He was prepared to be pleased with life in practically any circumstances and it is necessary to add that he was quite often as pleased with death.

He found the men and women in the world quite charming. He liked men in general and if, in particular, there was one here or there that he did not like, then, inevitably Mr. O'Mara found some way of dealing with the situation. He adored women. That is to say he adored the idea of women in general; was prepared to adore any woman in particular, providing she came up to certain standards; could be absolutely and entirely ruthless with a woman—if such process became necessary—in exactly the same manner as he could be quite ruthless with a man.

His eyes were of an attractive blue. His face, which was round, was fresh complexioned. He had an attractive moustache of the Ouida type, and his fair hair curled back from an intelligent forehead in waves which made most women envious. Mr. O'Mara was an exceedingly able person. He was one of those people who can do almost anything.

He played the piano, rode a horse, was a good shot, could sail a boat. He spoke a considerable number of languages, though very few people were aware of the fact. He had a nice taste in clothes which were always suited to his own peculiar characteristics. He had a quick, cool, mathematical—albeit whimsical—brain and was extremely apt with a hand gun.

Mr. O'Mara would charm you, would eat and drink with you, would converse with you, play cards with you, win your money off you, swear unfailing loyalty to you; and kill you; all with the same complete and dispassionate pleasure—a pleasure which was derived from the fact that Mr. O'Mara believed that anything that he did was for the good of the world in general and himself in particular.

These things being considered, it will easily be obvious that Mr. O'Mara was an ideal person to be employed by Mr. Quayle. He was, in fact, Quayle's star employee. Quayle, who had a sense of the obvious and intuition backed by a logical discernment that was probably unequalled, had realised, very quickly, certain things about O'Mara. These things were that O'Mara possessed an uncanny loyalty to the person for whom he worked, a brilliant personality, an utter and complete ruthlessness connected with all things German, all things Japanese. That there was some reason for this ruthlessness was apparent, but Quayle had not even been curious about causes. He was concerned only with effects.

O'Mara had a *flair* for picking up the pieces; for dealing with the job that had gone wrong; for stepping in on a business at the last moment and putting everything in its proper place.

O'Mara had worked for Quayle for a long time. What he failed to do by cleverness or by ruthlessness he did by luck. He had charm—and a certain softness which appeared only in his love for dumb animals—that he employed as a weapon.

Mr. O'Mara was unique, ubiquitous and certain. He was as sure as the hand of Death. If he took great pleasure in living it was because he was always prepared—at any moment—to be intrigued and amused at the prospect of dying—probably suddenly and very roughly.

O'Mara paused at the top of St. James' Street; stood for a moment watching the traffic, the women. He liked St. James' Street. He liked it all the more because it was over two years since he had seen it.

And he had covered a great deal of ground in those two years. He took from the breast pocket of his well-cut jacket a leather case; extracted a small black cigar, bit off the end, lit it, stood inhaling the strong smoke, at peace with and approving of the world.

He began to walk down St. James' Street. At the bottom he turned into Pall Mall, went into an office building, examined the address indicator. He found that the Overseas Air Conditioning Plant Company had its existence on the third floor. He went up in the lift.

In the large well-furnished outer office was the blonde girl, dressed in a neat coat and skirt, busily engaged at a typewriter. O'Mara smiled at her. She thought it was a lovely smile; and when he spoke she thought he had the most delightful voice; that it sounded rather like a caress. These things did not too greatly affect her mentality because she had heard about Mr. O'Mara.

He said: "My name's O'Mara. Believe it or not I've just come back from South America."

The girl came forward and raised the oak barrier. She said: "Please come in, Mr. O'Mara."

He followed her across the office. She opened the door on the other side, stood aside for him to go in.

Quayle was sitting at the big walnut desk in the corner of the large private office. The blonde girl closed the door quietly.

Quayle got up. He came round the desk, his hand outstretched. He said: "Hallo, Shaun. So you got back?"

"Yes, I'm back, Quayle," said O'Mara. "I had a very nice time, a very pleasant trip."

Quayle sat on the edge of the desk. They smiled at each other. O'Mara stood, his feet planted wide apart, looking like a handsome bull. The slightly rank odour of the Brazilian cigar permeated the office.

Quayle said: "So you're still smoking those things?"

"I've never found anything that suited me as well," said O'Mara. "They're restful and they don't last too long. They're like women ought to be but aren't."

Quayle said: "Yes? I take it by your attitude that everything is all right?"

O'Mara came closer to Quayle. He said: "Yes, it was very troublesome though." He knocked the ash off his cigar.

Quayle said. "Tell me."

O'Mara shrugged his shoulders. "He evidently knew what you'd decided about him," he said, "and it seems that he heard when I landed in South America. He went down to Rio. I knew he'd go to Rio. They always think they're safer in a big place. They think they can hide in a place like Rio. They think you won't see them in the crowd. And then, in Rio, there are lots of lovely women, lots of bright lights, lots of delightful drink. They can acquire Dutch courage cheaply in the evening—a process not particularly easy fifty miles outside the city."

Quayle asked softly: "Did you tell him why?"

O'Mara nodded. "I told him why," he said. "I told him he was a son of a bitch; that if he'd had any decency in his composition he would have killed himself before we had time to get around to him."

"Did you tell him what had happened because he talked?" asked Quayle.

O'Mara nodded again. "I told him," he said. His tone was delightfully conversational, charmingly casual. "I told him that as a result of his wanting to accept that six thousand pounds; of his deciding to give the information for which he got the six thousand pounds; two troop ships had been sunk; that we had lost a lot of men." He smiled a little. "He was filled with remorse," said O'Mara.

Quayle asked: "What happened?"

O'Mara walked to the fireplace. He dropped gracefully and easily for a man of his bulk into the big leather armchair.

He said: "I went into a little café in the Praça Maua, and there he was as large as life, drinking *Cachaça*." He smiled at Quayle. "*Cachaça's* dynamite. You probably know that. It's about the cheapest drink there is. You can get drunk on it more quickly than on anything I know of. But he didn't seem to be getting drunk so easily."

O'Mara sighed. He was remembering a picture. He was remembering the smell of the hot sun-baked, shimmering pavements, the vague aroma of coffee and tobacco from the nearby wharves and the little shops.

He went on: "I went over and talked to him. I talked to him like a father." O'Mara smiled charmingly again. "I told him that you couldn't run away from O'Mara at all."

Quayle asked: "What did he say when he knew what you were there for?"

O'Mara shrugged his shoulders. He said: "He tried everything he knew. He suggested all sorts of ways of making retribution. But I thought I'd have to get it over with as quickly as possible because he'd already got to the state of mind when in the evenings he was hanging about the *Mangue*—the native quarter. He was getting too fond of the coffee-coloured girls there. I thought he might get even more frightened; that he might do a little talking; that he might even go to the police. Naturally I didn't want that."

Quayle asked: "What did you do?"

O'Mara said casually: "I slipped a Micky Finn into a drink I bought him. Just as he was going to pass out I got him outside into the car. I drove him forty miles out. I found a charming place for him—a stinking swamp filled with yellow banana spiders and snakes." He smiled reminiscently. "I thought that would make an adequate resting place for him. I shot him and buried him."

Quayle said softly: "And that is the end of *that*. You're looking well, Shaun."

O'Mara said: "I'm feeling well. It's odd being back here after this long time. England's a wonderful place. I don't know any other country that can wear a war for so long and show so little."

Quayle asked: "Where are you staying?"

"I've got a flat," said O'Mara. "Quite a nice place—near Knightsbridge. Have you anything for me to do or am I on holiday?"

Quayle moved away from the desk. He put his hands in his pockets. He began to walk about the room. He said:

"Look, Shaun, don't get the wrong angle on this, because there isn't any comparison between this thing and the thing you've just done."

O'Mara said: "No?" He raised his eyebrows ever so slightly. He said: "You don't mean to tell me that somebody else has ratted?"

Quayle stopped. He shook his head. He stood in the centre of the room looking down at O'Mara.

He said: "No, not that." There was a pause; then he went on: "Shaun, you remember Ricky Kerr? He's done some good work in the last sixteen or seventeen months. He's a highly-strung type, you know—rather keen on women. Also it seems that he's been drinking a little lately."

O'Mara said: "Yes?"

Quayle went on: "He did a job a few days ago—a little thing that had to be done. He came to see me the next day and I gave him a list of agents I've got working in occupied France. He had to deliver it to Jerry Vining, who was being dropped from a plane the night after. Well, it seems that Kerr was suffering from a little reaction from the job—"

O'Mara interrupted: "I think that's very bad. I don't like people who have reactions."

Quayle said: "Maybe not, but everybody isn't like you, Shaun. *He* had one."

O'Mara said: "Well, what did he do, Peter? Tell me."

Quayle said: "He went off in the evening and he had a drink. He was picked up by a woman in a pub called the Green Headdress. He went off with her. He stayed the night and she had the list off him. He came to me the next morning and told me."

O'Mara said: "What an inconsiderate bastard. Why do they do things like that?" His tone was just a little peeved.

Quayle said: "I don't know, but he did it. There's the situation. I sent Vining off yesterday morning. He was dropped in France last night. And here's this woman walking around with this list. It's not very good."

O'Mara said: "Her walking around with it doesn't matter. It's what she's going to do with it. Can she get it over there? Can she get it to the enemy?"

Quayle said: "I don't know. The man who was their post-office—a very clever one—a man called Lelley—the man who normally got things out for them—was the fellow Kerr dealt with. So I don't know what she's going to do with the list. The trouble is that it's rather obvious that they were on to Kerr. Somebody knows something about him. I don't like that."

O'Mara said: "I bet you don't. That's dynamite." He sighed. "What do I have to do?" he said.

Quayle said: "The night he did the Lelley job, Kerr went to a party. I think somebody was on to him. Cordover, another of my people, who was working with Kerr, called through to him at that party. Whoever it was knew about him guessed what the thing was. They were able to get in touch with somebody else. That somebody else expected Lelley to be dealt with—they evidently didn't mind that if the process could put them in touch with us. Somehow they had a tail on Kerr. That would be easy enough if they saw him leave the country to come back to London, and it must be somebody who knows his characteristics—somebody who had an idea that he'd get a little cut after that job—somebody who knew that a damned good-looking woman could get away with it. Do you understand?"

"I'm beginning to," said O'Mara. "It looks to me like the old story. Someone ought to set it to music and make a gramophone record of it, except that I'm so tired of it."

Quayle went on: "I've acted quickly. Cordover, who's extremely reliable—a rather tough Cockney—a nice boy—has already done a lot. I've given him specific instructions, but he's not good enough to see this thing through on his own. I want you to handle it, Shaun. How's the memory?"

O'Mara said: "The memory's as good as ever it was."

"All right," said Quayle. "The party I'm talking about was thrown by a woman called Mrs. Glynda Milton. The other women there were Magdalen Francis, Therese Martyr, Elvira Fayle. Sandra Kerr—Ricky's wife—was also there. There was another interesting person there too—a Spaniard called Miguales."

O'Mara said: "I've got all that. Where do I go from here?"

Quayle said: "I'm going to ring Ricky. He's probably suffering from a fit of remorse at the moment. I don't think he feels quite so good about anything. I'll tell him you'll come and see him this evening. I suggest you have a heart-to-heart talk with him. I suggest you go into his association with all those beautiful ladies. He'll talk all right. Maybe you'll get on to something that he couldn't see. Maybe you'll sense something, Shaun. At least, you will if that headpiece of yours is working like it used to. Remember this—you can be as tough as you like. You can do what you want. Incidentally, you'll find Sammy Cordover a great help. Leave your address with the girl outside and I'll get him to get in touch with you. And she'll tell you where to find Ricky Kerr."

O'Mara drew on his black cigar. He said: "All that sounds very simple. There's just one point that occurs to me. The main idea seems to be that the other side knew that you'd be on to Lelley. They've used Lelley as a stooge to find out what you were doing, just as in the same way you've used Ricky Kerr as a stooge to get at them. So one thing's rather obvious, isn't it?"

Quayle asked: "What's obvious?"

O'Mara said: "They must know where Kerr lives." He smiled at Quayle.

Quayle returned the smile. He said: "You're quite right, Shaun. I knew you'd get on to that. They know where Kerr's flat is. They *must* know."

O'Mara said: "I like that. That gives me something to start from. I've got an idea. You know what it is. I think I can play it with Cordover."

Quayle said: "I think I know what you mean. It might be a start anyway."

O'Mara got up. He said: "All right. I suppose really I'm working against time. I suppose you want to get that list, Peter—before they get it out?"

Quayle grinned. He said: "I don't give a damn about the list! It was a fake list anyway. I had an idea that they were using Lelley as a stooge. They knew that we suspected Lelley. I had an idea they were going to lay for Ricky and I wasn't taking any chances. The list I gave him was phoney but he doesn't know it. The list that went down to Jerry Vining was the real one."

O'Mara said: "A clever person, aren't you, Peter? You never let anybody know what you're doing or what you're thinking. So you pulled a fast one on Kerr, and it was very lucky you did. Maybe you're making a stooge out of me." He shrugged his shoulders and grinned happily. "Nothing would surprise me about you," he said. "Well, I'll be getting along. I won't get in touch with you unless I've got to."

Quayle said: "No, Shaun. Keep away from here. I know you'll see this through. It's *very* important."

O'Mara stood in the doorway. He said: "Of course I shall see it through. I always do, don't I?"

He went out. In the outer office he left his address with the blonde girl. He said: "You'll always get me there if you want me." He looked at her with his clear blue eyes. She began to blush.

She wondered why. She came to the conclusion after he had gone that it must have been the way he said "want."

III

It was cold outside, but in O'Mara's flat in Knightsbridge there was an air of well-being—of comfort. The place looked as if it had been lived in, although he had only been there for a few days. He sat by the telephone table in a wine-coloured velvet dressing-gown, the receiver pressed close to his ear, listening to Sammy Cordover.

O'Mara liked the sound of Cordover. He liked the way the little Cockney talked, the method in which he presented his ideas.

He said: "That's all very nice, Sammy. I think you and I can do quite a job together. Now you've all the details, haven't you? I'm leaving here at nine o'clock. I shall look into the Berkeley Buttery and have a drink. I shall come outside the Berkeley Buttery and stand about on the pavement; then I'll walk down to Kerr's place." There was a pause. O'Mara went on: "Listen, Sammy, you're no fool. You're fond of Kerr, aren't you? You've done a lot of work with him. What do you think about him?"

Cordover said: "He's a great guy, Mr. O'Mara—a great guy. I know he is. But, you know, the best of us get tired. He's been drinking a little. Maybe his nerve got a bit worn—if you know what I mean."

O'Mara said: "I know what you mean, but in our game your nerve mustn't get worn. Does *your* nerve get worn, Sammy?"

Cordover laughed.

O'Mara said: "I'd like meeting you, Sammy. When we can meet we will. We'll have a drink together. I'd like to know how you got into this game."

Cordover's voice took on a new tone. It was a brittle hard tone. It sounded ominous. He said:

"I can tell you that now, Mr. O'Mara. My sister—her name was Rose—she was a swell girl, I'm tellin' you, Mr. O'Mara—she had class too—she wasn't like me; she was educated. And she was pretty. . . ."

O'Mara said: "Yes?" His voice was caressing. "So she's the reason you got into this game, Sammy. So *who* did *what* to *her*?"

Cordover said softly: "She was a nurse in the Stanley Hospital in Hong Kong, Mr. O'Mara."

It sounded to O'Mara as if the devil were speaking.

He said slowly: "I've got it, Sammy." He smiled into the telephone. "All right. We play it as arranged. I'll be seeing you." He hung up.

He got up, turned on the radio. He stood in front of the instrument listening to the music that came through. A good band was playing a rhumba. It reminded O'Mara of South America. He liked music. Like all Irishmen music did something to him; produced in him that extraordinary sense of exhilaration, the sense that led you to want to adventure, the sense that made you want to take chances; that gave you a kick out of taking chances.

After a while he took off the velvet dressing-gown, threw it across a chair, went into his bedroom. From a drawer he took a Luger pistol—rather an extraordinary affair. It was a normal Luger pistol with two inches cut off the barrel. Screwed on to the end of the shortened barrel was a bulbous-looking silencer. The thing had been made for O'Mara by a very clever gentleman in Rio—an individual who liked killing without too much noise. It was a nice job.

O'Mara put on his waistcoat and a double-breasted jacket. Inside the left side of the jacket which had been specially cut to allow for the weight, was a built-in pistol pocket. O'Mara put the Luger into the pocket, put on the jacket. He went back to the sitting-room, poured himself out a small glass of brandy. He held it up to the light, drank it. He lit another of his black cigars. He put on a well-cut blue overcoat, a black soft hat. He went out.

Half an hour afterwards he came out of the Berkeley Buttery. It was cold. O'Mara stood about on the pavement talking to the hall-porter who was trying to find him a cab. He flashed his torch rather ostentatiously. There was no cab available. He decided to walk.

He began to walk down Berkeley Street, his hands in his pockets, his cigar hanging out of the corner of his mouth, his black hat over one side of his head. If it had been light enough to see him, passers-by would have considered O'Mara to be a romantic figure.

He walked slowly, appreciating the cold tang in the air, the flavour of the cigar. He was thinking. He was thinking about a woman he had known in Rio. There was a piece. A real woman—that, thought O'Mara. He wondered if he would ever see her again.

Ten minutes afterwards he arrived at Kerr's flat, rang the doorbell; stood, his black hat in his hand, waiting patiently till the door was opened.

Ricky Kerr stood in the doorway. His slim figure showed against the light in the hall behind him.

O'Mara said softly: "Good-evening. Kerr, I believe? My name's O'Mara. Maybe somebody told you something about me?"

Kerr said: "Come in."

O'Mara left his coat and hat in the hall. He went into the sitting-room after Kerr. He stood just inside the doorway looking at Kerr.

Kerr said, with an odd smile: "I ought to have known Quayle better. I thought when I saw him this morning that, having blotted my copybook and been forgiven, this thing was more or less over. But of course it couldn't be."

O'Mara said—and when he spoke his voice was very soft and caressing and comforting: "You listen to me, Kerr. I've

been working for Quayle for a long time—all over the place—
all over the world. That one never lets his left hand know what
his right hand is at. Why should he? But you're all right. He
understands about you. But you realise he's got to *do* something about it. It's not a very *good* situation."

Kerr said: "Don't I know that? I don't have to tell you what
a heel I think I am. Would you like a drink?"

O'Mara said: "Yes. I'm fond of liquor."

Kerr said: "I've got some whisky." He mixed the drinks.

O'Mara sat down with the large glass of whisky in his hand.
He looked at Kerr for a long time. He said:

"You've taken a knock over this, haven't you? You don't
look too good. You need a rest." His voice was still caressing.

Kerr said: "It never rains but it pours. At the present
moment I'm in the doghouse every way. First of all I pull this
thing on Quayle, because I've been a damn' fool. And when I
got home to-day I found that my wife had decided to go off.
She's left me. I don't think I like *that* very much either."

O'Mara said: "Too bad. Wives do that sometimes, you know.
They get that way. What's the trouble? She just bored with
you—wives do get bored with people like us, you know—they
never know where we are—or is there anybody else?"

Kerr lit a cigarette. He said: "That's the annoying part about
it. There *is* somebody else."

O'Mara said: "Who?" He looked straight at Kerr.

Kerr drank some whisky. He said: "She's gone to a man
called Miguales—a Spaniard—rather a nice type. A tough
fellow—he fought in the Spanish war."

O'Mara said: "That's interesting. That would be the Miguales
who was at the party that you went to that night of the Lelley
business. Right?"

Kerr said: "Right." He laughed shortly. It was an odd laugh.
He said: "Quayle hasn't wasted any time, has he? So he's on
to that party. He thinks—"

O'Mara said: "Why should you worry about what he thinks? That party is important. You've got to realise that somebody was wise to you, Kerr. Somebody at that party. And now your wife goes off with Miguales, who was there."

Kerr said: "Listen, are you suggesting—"

O'Mara said softly: "I'm not suggesting anything. I'm stating facts. And you wouldn't get tough, would you, Kerr? It's too late to start being tough."

Kerr shrugged his shoulders. He said: "You're perfectly right. I've no right to be tough about anything."

There was a silence; then he said: "You haven't come here for nothing, O'Mara. You want to know something. You've seen Quayle?"

O'Mara said: "I've seen Quayle and I'm handling this job. When I take on a job I finish it." He smiled beatifically. "I see everything through to its logical conclusion. I'm going to see this thing through. I've come here because I'm going to ask you some questions. You're going to answer them. Probably you won't like them."

He laughed. It was a boyish laugh. It altered the atmosphere of the flat. It raised it from something dramatic to something rather amusing and bright. It even affected Kerr. He found himself smiling at O'Mara.

He said: "Well, I'll play ball. I've got to play ball." O'Mara said: "Can I have another drink?" He waited till Kerr handed the glass back to him; then he said:

"Listen, Ricky, you and I are such old hands at this game that we don't have to delude each other. You've slipped up. Well, it might have been me. There, but for the grace of God, goes Shaun O'Mara. It just didn't happen to be me. My business as far as possible is to put it straight. I'm the gentleman with the dustpan who goes round sweeping up the pieces. Now you give it to me straight. . . ."

Kerr said: "All right. I'll come clean."

He stood, leaning against the cocktail cabinet. He was thinking about Sandra, wondering where she was—what she was doing.

O'Mara settled himself back against the cushions in the big armchair. He took a sip of whisky and looked at Kerr over the edge of the glass. O'Mara was feeling happy. He was introducing himself to a problem which—eventually—he would solve; a problem which would resolve itself into a battle of wits, and possibly other things against somebody or something. And it was nice to be working in England once more.

He said: "Listen, Ricky. I'm interested in the party you went to on the night you fixed Lelley. I've had a certain amount of information about that party from Quayle. He hasn't wasted much time. All right . . . well, besides Miguales—the Spanish bloke—the one your wife goes for in such a big way" (O'Mara managed to convey a certain sorrow in his smile) "and the Fighting French officer, there were four women there, weren't there? They were Elvira Fayle, Therese Martyr, Glynda Milton—your hostess, and Magdalen Francis. Is that right?"

Kerr said: "Right."

O'Mara said: "If I know anything about men you're a hell of a man with women. I should think some of these women at this party had liked you a lot, hadn't they?"

Kerr said: "Maybe."

O'Mara said in a staccato voice: "Which ones—which ones had you slept with, Ricky?"

There was a pause; then Kerr said: "I suppose there's been a certain amount of funny business with most of them." He added quickly: "Don't think I'm *stuck* on any of them."

O'Mara said: "A man doesn't *have* to be *stuck* on a woman. Maybe she's got something that appeals to you—an ankle, a tone of voice, the way she does her hair, her hands, the way she walks." He went on: "By what I've heard of you, you're stuck on your wife, Ricky. I hear she's a lovely woman. But I understand. A man can be in love with a woman but he can slip up."

He laughed softly. "So there was something on between you and all of these women—at different times, I suppose? Just one of those things."

Kerr said: "Yes, just one of those things."

There was another silence.

O'Mara said: "Have you any reason to believe that any of these women might have had anything to do with the enemy? Of course not. If you'd had such an idea you'd have watched your step. But having regard to what's happened do you think there might have been something?"

Kerr shook his head. He said: "No. Listen, Glynda Milton is just—well, she's a nice woman. She loves throwing parties. She's temperamental. She falls for a man now and again—not often. Magdalen Francis is, well—just a fool. She's man mad. She thinks of nothing but dressing and making conquests. The Fayle woman—Elvira Fayle—well, she's a nice little thing. It took an awful lot of trouble to get anywhere with Elvira. And as for the Martyr piece . . ." He laughed.

O'Mara said: "What's the joke about the Martyr piece?"

"She's just one of those odd women. She doesn't look anything very much. She's flat-breasted—not very good-looking in the face, but the rest of her is strangely attractive. She dresses very well."

O'Mara said: "Why did you go for *her*? You sound as if you weren't even particularly interested."

Kerr said: "I don't know. There are a lot of things I don't know about women. There're a lot of things you don't know about them. She had a certain attraction and in a way I was sorry for her."

O'Mara said: "You were sorry for her, so you went out for her too?"

"Oh, something like that," said Kerr. "Does it matter?"

"Not an awful lot." O'Mara's voice was still casual. "I just wanted to get a picture."

He went on: "Stick around, Ricky. Don't go out too much. I'd like you to be here if I want to get in touch with you. I'll give you a ring within the next day or so."

Kerr said a little anxiously: "Do you think you can clean this up? Do you think you can put it right?" He went on: "I'm thinking about those fellows over in France—Vining and the rest of them. If somebody gets that list over there it's going to be pretty goddam bad for them."

O'Mara said: "That's true, I'm afraid. Still we'll do the best we can. By the way, Ricky—I'm afraid the question is a personal one, but I've got to ask it—what are you going to do about Mrs. Kerr? Are you going to see her or this fellow Miguales?"

Kerr shrugged his shoulders. "I'll do what you want," he said. "I don't want to start anything if it's going to be inconvenient. . . ."

O'Mara said: "Thanks. Just don't do anything at all for the moment. Indulge in a little masterly inactivity. You see, I'm interested in these other women who were at the party—at least I *think* I am—and I don't want you to do anything that's going to throw them into a huddle over a nice juicy scandal. When I've had a chance to try out this and that, well, then you can do what you like."

Kerr shrugged his shoulders again. He was thinking that when you lost a thing you lost it. It didn't much matter what you did about it afterwards.

O'Mara looked at the end of his cigar. Then he put it back into his mouth and inhaled the pungent smoke with obvious pleasure.

He leaned forward. He said: "Now, Ricky, let you and me have a heart-to-heart talk about these women. Let's hear all about them, how they dress, what they like, what they don't like, how they amuse themselves. Let's start with Elvira Fayle. Let's hear all about her. Now, first of all . . ."

O'Mara began his subtle cross-examination.

*

Sandra Kerr stood looking down into the fire. One hand held a cigarette; the other was stretched out towards the flames. The warmth from the fire came up toward her, encompassed her, gave her a feeling of pleasure. Or did it? Was it something else that was responsible for her strange sense of elation? She thought: This is going to hurt Ricky . . . all this. But he had it coming to him. I hope it's going to be good for him—some day. When he grows up. Poor Ricky. . . .

She wore a sapphire-blue tailored corded velvet frock. At her throat was a lace scarf of dusty pink caught with a sapphire brooch.

She threw the cigarette into the fire, walked slowly up and down the room, her hands clasped behind her. She was thinking of Ricky; of Miguales; of people. She was thinking all sorts of interesting things. She was thinking that half the fun in life consisted in trying to work out what was going to happen; then watching it happen; seeing where you were wrong.

At one end of Miguales' sitting-room was a long mirror. She looked at herself in the mirror. She thought that the way her hair was dressed and tied back with a blue ribbon was attractive. She wondered if Miguales would think it was attractive. She hoped he would.

A strange man, she thought. She smiled a little. She stopped walking about the room, went to a corner where a telephone stood on a table. The telephone cord ran from the instrument down to the wainscoting. She went away; came back in a minute with a sharp penknife. Very carefully, cautiously, she unravelled the wires inside the telephone cord, taking them apart with the tiny blade of the knife. When she had finished she tested the telephone. It was dead. There was no connection.

She heard a key in the lock; closed the penknife; slipped it into the pocket of her frock; went back to the fire. When Miguales came in she was standing there, relaxed, reposeful, one arm stretched casually along the mantelpiece.

He stood just inside the doorway looking at her. There was a dejected stoop to his shoulders and his long virile hands hung by his side almost in an attitude of despair. He stood looking at her for a long time as if he were trying to analyse his own thoughts of her.

She said: "Good-evening, Enrico. Why are you so unhappy?" Her voice was very soft, very low.

Miguales shrugged his shoulders. He went to the sideboard, mixed and poured out two cocktails. He came across to where she stood, the cocktail glasses in his hands. He gave her one.

He said: "Never was there a more extraordinary affair than ours, my beloved. Never was there anything quite so incomprehensible—so almost stupid. Never was there anything that began so wonderfully and that will end—as I feel it must end—so tragically."

Sandra said with a smile: "You're depressed, Enrico. You've been unhappy for days. You're worrying about my husband—what he thinks—what he's going to do. You're worrying about him. Why don't you relax? Believe me, Ricky will be sensible. He always is, you know."

Miguales said: "I don't think so. Do you think he's been very sensible about *you*?"

She shrugged her shoulders. She drank some of the cocktail, put the glass on the mantelpiece behind her. She said:

"That's different. You must understand that Ricky has always been very fond of me, but most of the time he's been fighting a battle—a battle between his own temperament and himself. I told you when I came to you that I was very fond of Ricky. I told you that I didn't think there was going to be a great deal in it for you, Enrico. But because Ricky's been stupid about women; been drinking too much; been behaving generally in a foolish way that I was disinclined to put up with; that doesn't mean that he's stupid—in any event not stupid enough to do anything *really* foolish."

Miguales finished his drink. He went to the sideboard, poured another one. She noticed that his hand was shaking a little.

He said: "I'm not afraid of Ricky. Why should I be? I just hate life—that's all. I thought I'd got something. I thought I was going to make a success of my mission in this country. I thought I should be here for some time; that when I went back to Spain I should take you with me as my wife. Those thoughts gave me a great deal of pleasure."

She said: "And now? Don't they give you any pleasure now?"

He turned. He stood leaning against the sideboard, looking at her. He asked:

"How did you first come to a conclusion about me, Sandra?"

She said: "I was talking to Therese one day. Therese has always been my very good friend. I'm fond of her, and she is very fond of me. She was unhappy and miserable because she knew what was going on between Ricky and some other women who were friends of hers. Therese didn't like that. It took a great deal of courage on her part to tell me what she had to tell. Then somehow—I don't know how—your name came into the conversation. She told me that you loved me; that you had said if I were your wife you would be contented with whatever I wanted to give."

She shrugged her shoulders. She went on: "Well, I wanted to get away from Ricky. I had to. You must understand, Enrico, that a woman can be so fond of a man that she can still go on putting up with what he does, even although she feels she's losing her self-respect in the process. It was necessary that I should make up my mind quickly. I made it up. I spoke to you." She smiled at him. "And here we are."

Miguales stood quite motionless. He said: "You are the most lovely person I have ever seen in my life. I don't think I've ever known anybody as beautiful as you are or one who is so kind. How strange it all is. I wonder which of your friends would believe that during the days that you have been with me there has been nothing between us; that I have never even kissed you. I wonder if they could understand that such a communion of the spirit was possible."

She asked: "Does it matter what they believe? One day perhaps, Enrico, everything may be possible between us. In the meantime tell me something . . . what is troubling you?"

He said in a low voice: "A terrible thing has happened. My mission in this country is a failure. As you know I came here representing the Spanish National Government. I came here more or less as an expert in propaganda to try and create a situation between my own country and yours, in which something would be possible." He shrugged his shoulders; spread his hands in a hopeless gesture. "Well, nothing is possible. How could it be possible? Franco is associated in the minds of the English people with the Germans. Whoever I speak to, believes that I am hand in glove with the Germans too; that the Spanish Government is pro-German. I have realised that it is impossible for me to persuade them to the contrary.

"But I had hoped that I should be here long enough for your divorce to have gone through; to have married you in this country; to have taken you back to Spain. Well, now that is impossible."

Sandra stiffened. She said: "Enrico!"

He nodded. He said bitterly: "It's true, Sandra. I have been given my *congé*. I have been practically ordered by the British Government to leave this country within the next four or five days. Well . . . what do we do now?"

She said: "My God! What do *I* do, Enrico?"

He said: "That is what has been worrying me so much. For myself I do not care. I am thinking only of you."

She said: "Can't I go to Spain? Can't I . . ."

He interrupted: "No, they won't let you go. They won't give you an exit permit to go to Spain. Why should they? Do you think they don't know that you're here with me in my flat now?"

Sandra sighed. She looked at him. Her violet eyes were dark, unhappy. She said: "What are we to do, Enrico?"

He said: "I don't know. I wish to God I did know. Money—that's all right. I can leave you any money that you want. I have plenty, but I must go back to Spain. I don't even know when I shall see you again."

There was a silence. Then she said: "Listen, I think we're both very sad to-night—both very unhappy. Well, we have to do something about this. We have to make a decision, but don't let's try to make it to-night. Let's do nothing. Let's talk about it to-morrow. Let's go somewhere and dine now and dance and pretend. Let's pretend that none of these things has happened? Shall we do that?"

He smiled at her. He said: "You're wonderful, aren't you? You have a *flair* for getting the best out of life. That is because you are so good. Because of that you can be happy." He moved away from the sideboard. He said: "We will do as you say. Will you ring up for a table?"

She said: "Yes." She went to the telephone. As she took up the instrument, she said: "Give yourself another drink, Enrico, and smile for me. The world hasn't come to an end. Who knows—there may be something wonderful round the corner, waiting for both of us."

He poured out another cocktail.

Sandra said: "There's something wrong with this telephone. I can't get a dialling tone."

He came to her. He said: "Let me try." He took the instrument, tried it. He said: "It's quite dead."

She said: "Don't bother. I'll go down to the porter's lodge. I'll telephone the exchange and ask them to send round in the morning. I'll engage our table from there. Have your drink. I'll be back in a minute."

Downstairs just within the entrance hall, the little glass-fronted porter's lodge was empty. Sandra went in. She took up the telephone, dialled a number. After a moment she said:

"I'm speaking for Mr. Miguales in Flat No. 22 at St Ervins Court, St. John's Wood—Primrose 73624. Something's gone wrong with the telephone, I'm afraid, and it is essential that it should be repaired quickly. Señor Miguales, by the way, has a diplomatic passport. I thought you'd like to know that."

A voice said: "Very well. We'll send round in the morning, Ma'am, as soon as we can."

She said thank you and hung up. She waited a moment: then she dialled the number of the restaurant; engaged the table for dinner.

Sammy Cordover stood in a dark doorway opposite the entrance of Kerr's apartment block. He stood leaning against the wall, his hands in his pockets, relaxed. He was thinking about O'Mara.

He thought that O'Mara would be a big guy. Something very special. He could tell that by the way O'Mara spoke; by the timbre of his voice; by the controlled authority of his speech.

O'Mara . . . a hell of a name, thought Cordover. It *sounded* like something. There was something about a name like that. If a man had a name like O'Mara he had to be good . . . damned good.

Well . . . Sammy grinned to himself . . . there were plenty of opportunities for being good in the game they were in. You were telling *him*!

Just for a few seconds, from the other side of the street, he had seen O'Mara when he came out of the Berkeley Buttery; had identified him by the light of the torch which O'Mara had flashed so ostentatiously. So *that* was O'Mara.

It was cold, but Cordover did not feel the cold. He stood, his eyes fixed on the dark doorway opposite, waiting for someone to come out. If, as O'Mara thought, the other side had the Kerr flat under observation, that observation must be carried out from inside the building. They must keep an eye on the actual flat; must see who went in, pick them up when they came out. He moved a little; wished he could smoke a cigarette.

Three or four minutes went past; then the big doors on the other side of the road opened. The black-out curtain was parted and a man came out. Just for a moment, as he stood in the splash of light, Cordover saw him clearly. He was tall, thin, young. His face was thin and very white. The eyes were sunk deeply into his head. Vaguely his face reminded Cordover of that of a skeleton seen in a half light.

The man crossed the road. Cordover could hear the footsteps coming towards him. They stopped a few yards away. He began to grin. The man, who was obviously waiting for O'Mara to come out, had parked himself in one of the doorways to the left of the one in which Cordover was hidden. He said to himself: Well, whoever you are, pal, I don't think it's going to be very good for you. I think you're just another punk . . . just another one of the Lelley smart boys. He leaned back against the wall.

Ten minutes went by; then the door on the other side of the road opened again. O'Mara came out. He stood on the edge of the pavement, re-lighting his cigar; taking a great deal of time in the process. Then he turned to the right, walked slowly away.

Cordover waited until he heard the footsteps leave the doorway on his left; then he moved, walking silently after the footsteps. He thought: This is damned funny. It's almost like a procession.

The man who was following O'Mara knew his business. Aided by the darkness he kept fairly close to his prey, walking on the inner side of the pavement by the edge of the houses. He varied the tempo of his steps from time to time. He was well trained.

Now O'Mara began to increase his pace a little. He walked across Berkeley Square into Charles Street. The street was quiet and deserted. O'Mara crossed the road, turned into Queen Street, turned again, entered a Mews.

Cordover heard the footsteps in front of him quicken. He thought: You bloody fool . . . this is where you try it! He imagined the man in front putting his hand in his pocket, gripping the pistol that he thought he was going to use on O'Mara. . . .

The Mews was long and silent. It was filled with empty houses and garages. Even by day it was a desolate place.

Cordover began to quicken his steps. He advanced silently towards the sound of the feet in front of him. As the man turned into the Mews, Cordover was almost on his heels, and when he was well round the corner Cordover was upon him. He slipped his arm through that of the white-faced man, pressed a short automatic against the rough overcoat.

He said: "Take it easy, pal. Don't get excited or anything, will you?"

The man turned and looked at Cordover. A few yards away was a shaded street lamp. Cordover could see that the man's face was unaffected—almost as if he regarded such processes as being natural.

He said quietly: "I don't understand."

Cordover said: "You will. Come on."

They walked down the Mews. Twenty yards away O'Mara stood in the doorway of one of the empty houses. He had opened the door. He stood just inside the dark hallway.

He said: "Bring him in, Sammy."

The white-faced man said: "I think there's some mistake. I think—"

O'Mara said casually: "We might have made a mistake. If we have it's too bad."

They went inside. Cordover closed the door quietly behind them. O'Mara flashed on a torch. Quite obviously, he knew this house; must have investigated the lay-out between the time he had left Quayle and the time that Cordover spoke to him. He led the way down the stairs to a basement. There was only one blacked-out window.

O'Mara found a switch. He switched on a dim electric light. The room was dusty and bare except for two rickety chairs and a table.

O'Mara said to the white-faced man: "Make yourself at home, my friend!"

The man sat down. He put his hands on his knees and sat there looking at O'Mara. His deep-set eyes were burning.

O'Mara said to Cordover: "All right, Sammy. I'll handle this. You know what to do, don't you?"

Cordover said: "Yes. When?"

O'Mara said casually: "In a quarter of an hour, I should think. Not later. So long." He took the Luger pistol from its pocket.

Cordover went away.

O'Mara came over. He stood looking down at the man. He thought he was about twenty-eight years of age. He had taken his hat off; put it on the table. His hair was blonde and wavy. There was a scar on one side of his face.

O'Mara said: "Get up."

When the other obeyed, O'Mara ran his hands over his pockets. He found a .38 automatic pistol. He put it in his coat pocket; motioned the man back to the chair.

He said: "Well . . . that's that. So you thought you were going to finish me off. I suppose your boss thought that *somebody* would be going to see Kerr when it was known that he'd lost that list. Somebody important. Somebody like me!" O'Mara smiled pityingly. "You know," he went on smoothly: "I think someone's been making a fool of you. You're what the Americans call the fall guy."

The man said: "Yes?" A little smile played about his mouth. There was a silence; then he went on: "What happens now?"

O'Mara took the other chair, shook some of the dust off it, sat across it. He sat looking at the other for a long time, weighing him up, assessing him.

He said: "Listen, you and I don't have to waste a lot of time talking. Possibly you don't want to talk?"

The young man said: "There isn't anything I want to talk about." His English was perfect.

O'Mara said: "I don't suppose there is, but it might be a good thing if you talked. Who put you in to keep Kerr's flat under observation? Who are you working for?"

There was a pause, then the young man called O'Mara by a name—an obscene name. Then he sat still looking straight in front of him.

O'Mara smiled. He said: "A conventional pupil of one of Mr. Himmler's schools, hey? So you've decided to die for the Fuehrer and Fatherland without talking. You know it might be easier for you if you talked."

There was no reply.

O'Mara said casually: "I don't like you. I don't like your type. You make me sick. But I think I ought to tell you this. If you like to say what you know; if you like to tell me everything you know, I'll hand you over to one of our Service Departments and you can take a chance as to what they'd do with you. Well, what about it?"

There was no reply. The eyes that looked at O'Mara from out of their deep caverns in the young man's face were almost expressionless—apparently disinterested.

O'Mara sighed. He got up from the chair. He said: "Well, you have it your way."

The Luger, with the snub-nosed silencer on it, was in his right hand. O'Mara levelled the pistol; fired three times. The noise sounded like corks being drawn from bottles.

The young man fell sideways off the chair. He was dead when he fell. He lay on the floor looking rather like a dishevelled sack—a heap of brown overcoat.

O'Mara put the pistol back in his pocket. He went over to the figure, turned it over, opened the coat. He flapped open the underneath jacket and waistcoat with practised hands, taking no notice of the large ominous stain that was spreading all over the shirt beneath. He began to go through the pockets. He found two keys, some loose change, the stub-end of a pencil, in the waistcoat pockets. There was nothing in the trouser pockets. In the inside pocket of the overcoat was an envelope.

O'Mara took it out, looked at it. There was nothing written on the envelope but inside was a sheet of good notepaper. The note was written in Spanish and O'Mara noticed that it had been addressed to Señor somebody or other, but the name had been erased. Holding it under the light he could see the marks made by the erasure. He read the note. It said:

"Dear Señor—

"I do not think that you are being very kind to me. I do not think that you are giving me the sort of bargain which we agreed. I have done what I said I would do because I always keep my word, and now when the time comes for you to do your part it seems that I am to be left in the cold. I do not like this. I do not like it at all.

"I hope to find some means of seeing you and of settling this business in an amicable manner. I hope this will be possible. If not there is only one thing I can do. I should not like to do that because I am a man of honour.

"I hope and expect to hear from you within the next four days. I find myself in the most difficult position.

"E. M."

O'Mara sat down on the dusty chair. He held the note before him, read it and re-read it. He thought the handwriting was good. After a while he put the note back in the envelope, put it in his pocket. He rested his head on his hand, sat there looking steadily at the heap that lay on the floor. By now the red patch had begun to soak through into the overcoat.

Suddenly O'Mara began to smile. He said to himself: Well, I'll be damned! He seemed almost happy.

The door opened. Cordover came into the room. He said:

"It's all right. The truck's outside. I've got a fruit box we can use for that—an' some sacks." He nodded towards the heap on the floor.

O'Mara took out his cigar-case. He selected a cigar, lit it. He said: "That's excellent. We'll take it away. You know where it's to go?"

Cordover nodded. He said: "That's all fixed, Mr. O'Mara."

O'Mara went to the door. As he passed Cordover, he said, looking at the heap: "There's one for your sister. Maybe with luck, we'll score a couple more before this is through."

They went down the passage.

IV

Sammy Cordover, driving a small official van with the words "London Telephone Service" painted on the side of it, drew up outside St. Ervin's Court, got out of the van, went inside. He was dressed in overalls, carried a tool kit.

He said to the porter: "There's something wrong with the telephone at No. 22, I think."

The porter said: "Yes—Mr. Miguales on the first floor. It's just up the stairs and round the corner."

Cordover said: "Thanks."

He took the half-smoked cigarette from the corner of his mouth, stubbed it out, put the stub behind his left ear. He went upstairs, rang the bell of No. 22.

The maid opened the door.

Cordover said: "Telephone Service. You've got a phone wrong here, haven't you?"

She said: "Yes. Come in."

He followed her into the sitting-room, put down his tool kit, went over to the instrument. He said to the maid:

"I think somebody's been jiggling about with the connection—probably pulled the cord a bit too hard."

He opened his tool kit, began work.

Sandra Kerr came into the room. The maid said:

"Oh, Ma'am, this man's from the Telephone Service. He's mending it."

Sammy looked over his shoulder at Sandra. He said: "Good-morning."

She said: "Good-morning. Is it anything very difficult?"

"Oh no," said Sammy. "A few minutes' work."

She said: "Very well, Mary." The maid went out of the room.

Cordover, kneeling on the ground, continued with his work. He was fitting a new piece of flex, re-wiring the break. She came over to him. She said: "What actually was the matter with the telephone?"

He said: "I should think somebody has been playing about with the flex. They've broken the connection. It's nothing much."

He put one hand on the small table beside him. Between the knuckles was a small folded piece of paper. She slipped her hand over his, took the piece of paper.

She said: "Well, I'm glad it's not worse than that. If you want some coffee when you've finished the maid will give you some."

She went out of the room. In her bedroom she unfolded the piece of paper. It said:

"32 Fayle Street, Fulham Road—to-night, ten o'clock."

She went to the mantelpiece, put the piece of paper in an ashtray, put a match to it, watched it burn.

The Yellow Cantaloupe Club—an attractive *boite* not a hundred miles from Berkeley Square—presented a rarefied and sometimes enthralling atmosphere which had never failed to attract Mrs. Glynda Milton until to-night. And if, at the moment, she found herself unable to appreciate anything to any degree of satisfaction it was not because she desired such a situation but because of events over which she had no control.

Mrs. Glynda Milton was characteristic of a certain type of extremely good-looking woman who, in the fifth year of the war, finds herself unable to "take it."

There are many such women. She had a husband, who loved her and whose suspicions were easily aroused, an adequate allowance, a delightful flat, a superb wardrobe. She had everything that could make for what most women would call happiness. She was unhappy because she was bored. Because she was bored, she did things intended to relieve boredom. Things which, strangely enough, seemed only to accentuate it.

Glynda had *affaires* with such gentlemen as she considered worthy of the honour; she drank a little too much; she smoked too much; she spent too much. If she found the days too long it was because the nights were inevitably shorter.

She was slim and charming—with delightful hands and feet, and was one of those ladies who seemed to exist mainly for the purpose of gracing a chromium-legged high stool in a chromium-plated bar in one of the thousands of chromium-plated "clubs" which abound in the metropolis.

And if she needed an excuse for any of these things—if one were indicated—she had it pat. The reason was Mr. Hitler and The War and the fact that one was "browned off" by the process of having to stay put in London doing a little drinking in the aforementioned surroundings instead of rushing about the Continent from one *plage* to another, at the right times, in the right clothes, doing a little drinking in other, if similar, surroundings where you ordered your drink in some other language and where the young men were *very* passionate even if they were also financial-minded.

Of such was the kingdom of Glynda.

Now she sat at her table in the corner of the attractively furnished dining-room of the Yellow Cantaloupe whose subdued lights were so kind to the complexions of the charming ladies who inhabited the place, that the ladies themselves were often more kind than they had originally meant to be.

She was, as always, perfectly dressed. On the other side of the table, eating a cherry on a stick which she had taken from her cocktail glass, Therese Martyr, superb in an expensive but simple black frock—created by a *maestro*—with a single string of real pearls, regarded the club, Mrs. Milton and the world in general with generous approval.

Glynda Milton thought bitterly: You're very happy, Therese, aren't you? You're awfully pleased with yourself. I think I'd like to cut your throat, you bitch!

These thoughts, however, did not alter the expression of her face.

She said: "Therese, I want another cocktail, please, and I hope dinner won't be too long."

Therese Martyr signalled a hovering waiter, ordered the cocktail. She said: "Dinner will be here in a minute, my dear, I ordered a special one. We're going to have a chicken. I thought we ought to have a little celebration."

Her friend asked: "Why?"

Therese shrugged her shoulders. "I don't know," she said. "Anyhow, why should there be any particular reason. Of course, you know that you're looking quite radiant to-night, don't you, Glynda? And I love your frock. But then you have such exquisite taste in clothes."

Mrs. Milton thought: To hell with my taste in clothes.

She was frightened—terribly frightened. Periodically, her eyes moved to the door which led from the bar to the dining-room. She was waiting for someone to come through that door. She was waiting for a very large, quite charming, individual who terrified her, to come through the door. She was waiting for Mr. O'Mara.

She thought life was very strange and not a bit funny. This morning she had been almost happy. She had enjoyed going to the hairdresser. Her appointment there had been entirely successful. She came out of the place with the pleasurable feeling that enfolds a woman when her hair has been well dressed. Her taxicab, faithful because of the inordinate tip which Mrs. Milton inevitably paid, stood at the kerb.

But she had not reached it. From somewhere in the neighbourhood, between herself and the cab, had appeared the large well-dressed figure of Mr. O'Mara. He had smiled at her, had taken off his hat with rather a flourish that seemed a little foreign to her.

He had said: "Mrs. Milton, I believe? My name's O'Mara. I'm awfully sorry to pounce on you like this so unexpectedly, but I think you and I ought to have a little talk."

She had said: "Really! I don't think I know you." She had made a movement as if she were going to pass on.

O'Mara had said: "You *don't* know me, Mrs. Milton, but don't make any mistake about it, you're *going* to know me. You can get into your cab if you like, but I think it would be much more clever of you if you came with me and had coffee and a little talk."

She had said with a touch of indignation: "*Why* should I come with you and have coffee and talk. Why *should* I?" While she spoke she was racking her brains in an endeavour to remember where—if ever—she had met this large, well-dressed, rather overpowering person . . .

At that moment she had begun to feel frightened.

O'Mara had said with a pleasant smile: "I'll tell you why. You know that Hubert—your husband—is a little bit fed up with your gallivanting about. Now, isn't he? You know that just now he's in a frame of mind when he could be *very* nasty. And you can bet, my dear, that he'd be goddamned nasty if I were to let him know about some of those interesting nights that you spent with Ricky Kerr. Hubert would be *awfully* pleased, wouldn't he? He'd probably take you apart just to see what made you tick over . . . hey? So let's go and have the coffee and the talk, you silly little fool!"

Thus Mr. O'Mara . . . who could sound very rude, very ominous.

Therese Martyr said: "Here's your cocktail, dear. Oh . . . darling, have you heard the latest definition of a meteorologist?"

Glynda drank the cocktail in a gulp. She said she hadn't.

"A meteorologist," said Therese, happily, "is a man who looks in a woman's eyes and sees whether . . ."

Mrs. Milton said: "How good . . . how *very* good." But she was thinking of O'Mara. Standing there, on the pavement, looking up at him, at the smiling, fresh impertinent face, at the mouth that had just called her a silly little fool, she had thought: So this is blackmail. This is how it begins. Oh, my God!

She had said something like that.

O'Mara, still smiling, had continued: "Don't worry, Mrs. Milton. Nobody's going to blackmail you or frighten you—well, not much—providing you do what you're told. Now will you take your cab or shall *we* use it to go somewhere where we can get some coffee?"

She had said shortly: "Very well."

She had gone; they had coffee. And now she was waiting for Mr. O'Mara. Having been primed in what she was to say; drilled in what she was to say, she was waiting for Mr. O'Mara . . . wondering what the next thing would be; wondering if she would have to do other things, play other parts.

Therese Martyr said: "I've never known you drink a cocktail like that before. You just swallowed it in one gulp. Don't tell me you're taking to drinking?" She smiled playfully.

Mrs. Milton said: "I didn't notice. I'm a little perturbed—a little worried."

Therese said: "No?" She raised her eyebrows. "Don't tell me you've something really to worry about, Glynda. Can I know about it?"

"You know about it already," said Mrs. Milton. "Damned well you do. I'm worried about Sandra."

Therese raised her pencilled eyebrows again. She asked: "But why? Why should *you* worry about Sandra?"

Mrs. Milton said: "Because I think you've played a stinking trick on her." Her eyes blazed. "Because I think she's in a devil of a position. She happens to be a friend of mine, you know.

I'm really her friend and I don't mean *your* sort of friendship either, Therese."

Therese smiled. It was rather a pitying sort of smile. She said: "You're being very rude for a guest, aren't you, Glynda? Whatever are you talking about? Do you know?"

Glynda Milton said: "Listen. I know you've made a fool of yourself with Ricky Kerr. I know you were his mistress and he threw you over, didn't he? He got tired of you, so you had to do something about it. So you schemed to be revenged on him. And you brought that suave Spaniard, Miguales, along, told Sandra an awful lot of lies about Ricky, worked her up into the most fearful rage against him, and then flung her into the arms of Miguales, who was waiting to receive her."

Therese said: "Dear ... dear ... dear! Doesn't this all sound terrible?" There was a sardonic note in her voice. "And you're fearfully concerned about her?" she went on. "But why, my dear girl? It might surprise you to know that Miguales intends to marry Sandra. I think they'll make a wonderful couple."

Glynda Milton said: "Therese, you're a liar."

"Really!" said Therese. She was quite unperturbed.

"Oh yes, you are," Mrs. Milton went on. "Of course you wouldn't know that the business on which Miguales came to this country is over; that his mission has been a failure; that he's got to leave within two or three days' time; that it's quite *impossible* for him to marry Sandra."

She laughed bitterly. "She's got to get a divorce first, you know. And, quite candidly, I shouldn't think that Ricky would be very keen on making the process easy for her—not after the way he's been treated."

Therese Martyr said seriously: "Is all this true, Glynda? This is really rather terrible. Is it true that Miguales is leaving? But I thought he was going to be here permanently. I thought—"

Glynda Milton said: "Whatever you thought you were wrong. That's the position. Why couldn't you *wait* a little? But of course you couldn't. You had to be revenged on Ricky even if it meant making Sandra permanently unhappy. What's she to do now? She's left Ricky and she can't go back to him. And Miguales is going off. My God! What a situation."

Therese said casually: "I agree, Glynda. It's not a very good situation. Incidentally, where did you hear all this?"

Glynda lied glibly. She had learned her part well. She said: "Sandra telephoned me this morning. She told me."

Therese asked: "And did she tell you that Ricky had had an *affaire* with me? Did she tell you that?"

Glynda shook her head. "No," she said. "Ricky told me that. I telephoned him after I'd spoken to Sandra. I don't think he's feeling awfully well disposed towards you, Therese. Why should he? What a nasty little beast you've been to everybody."

Therese smiled. She said: "My dear, you always exaggerate. If I were you I should have another cocktail and relax."

Glynda Milton said: "I think you're quite right. In any event I don't believe in quarrelling publicly."

"Don't you?" said Therese sweetly. "I was beginning to think you did, my dear." She ordered another cocktail.

Glynda Milton looked towards the door. She shuddered a little inside. Through the door had come the large and smiling figure of Mr. O'Mara. She thought to herself: Well, here he is. I've done what he told me. Now perhaps I'll be safe . . . perhaps . . .

O'Mara stood just inside the entrance to the dining-room. His eyes wandered round the room, stopped on Mrs. Milton. A smile of surprise and satisfaction appeared on his face. He came quickly across to the table. He said:

"Well, if it isn't little Glynda—and after all these years."

She looked at him. After a moment, as if she recollected, she smiled. She said: "Shaun, where *have* you been? Oh, by the way, Therese, this is Mr. O'Mara—a very old friend of mine . . . Miss Therese Martyr."

O'Mara threw a smile at Therese. He said to Glynda: "I've been in South America working for the Ministry of Supply.

And am I glad to get back. You know it's all very well to be out of this war, and the Argentine is a marvellous place, but give me London."

Mrs. Milton said: "I'm very glad to see you back, Shaun. You look the same as you always did—perfectly pleased with yourself and the world in general."

He asked: "Why not? By the way," he went on, "how are all my friends? How are Ricky and Sandra?"

Mrs. Milton said dubiously: "Well . . ." There was a pause. "Ricky's working in the Ministry of Supply now," she said.

O'Mara asked: "How is he?"

"He's all right," said Mrs. Milton. "I suppose you'll be seeing him soon, won't you?"

"When I have time," said O'Mara. "I want to get settled down first and have a look at one or two of the spots in England I've always liked; then I'll get around to people."

A waiter came to the table. He said: "Excuse me, Mrs. Milton. There's a telephone call for you."

"Oh dear," said Glynda Milton. "I never get a moment's peace."

She went away.

Therese Martyr said: "Won't you sit down, Mr. O'Mara?"

"Thank you," said O'Mara. He pulled up a chair, sat down at the table. He said to the waiter: "I'll have a double Martini, please."

He looked at Therese appreciatively.

She said: "So you know the Kerrs?"

He nodded. "I've known Ricky for years," he said. "An awfully nice fellow—a bit volatile, you know, but very sound at heart. A great fellow. I'm very fond of him. I suppose you know them well?"

Therese said: "Yes, I know them very well. You know, there's been a little trouble there."

O'Mara raised his eyebrows. "No!" he said. "That astounds me. I'm very sorry to hear it. But it can happen, you know— even in the best regulated family."

Glynda Milton came back. She said: "Believe it or not I'll have to go. Hubert's just telephoned me from home. He's going off to the country somewhere and wants me back at once. So, like a dutiful wife, I must go."

Therese said: "Aren't you even going to wait for dinner, Glynda?"

"My dear, how can I?" said Glynda. "You know what Hubert is. He's always complaining that I dine out every night, and I believe I actually told him I was going to be in to-night. I must go." She looked at O'Mara. "Perhaps Mr. O'Mara would like to eat my chicken," she said.

Therese Martyr said: "That would be very nice. Why don't you, Mr. O'Mara?"

He looked at her. The admiration in his eyes was quite obvious. He said: "You know, Miss Martyr, I'm a very lucky man. This is my first night in London and I find myself dining with a beautiful woman. One of those sudden and unexpected surprises that make life so delightful. Glynda, I feel under an obligation to Hubert. I think it was marvellous of him to ring you up."

She said: "Well, put it to my credit. I really must be going. Good-night, Therese. So sorry to leave you. Good-night, Shaun. Come and see us some time."

She went out of the dining-room, through the bar, into the club vestibule. She waited there miserably while the commis- sionaire tried to get her a cab.

She thought: I hope I did what he wanted. Now perhaps he'll leave me alone. . . .

She was uncertain, unhappy. She was scared stiff. Scared of Mr. O'Mara, his schemes, his fake telephone calls, his threats, his smile—of everything about him. Somewhere inside her was an instinctive feeling that Mr. O'Mara was an ill wind that would do nobody any good.

The commissionaire got her a cab. She went home.

For once she was glad to be going home.

Sandra turned into the dark street; flashed her torch on to the door of the first house, worked out where Number 32 would be, hastened towards it.

She was thinking of Ricky; wondering what he was doing, what he was thinking. She was unhappy.

She felt that danger, like the darkness in the street, encompassed her. She felt that the time had come for some climax—some crisis which would be shattering. She hurried because she desired to know quickly such things as she *could* know and because she wished that the climax—whatever it might be—and its results, could be met, experienced, relegated to the past.

She arrived at the house. It was small, uninteresting, one of a long row of houses, each with a small garden in front and a few steps leading to the front door. The houses were Victorian, had been built in times of security and lower middle-class respectability.

She knocked at the door and waited. After a minute she heard steps inside. The door opened and she stepped into the dark hall. She heard the door close behind her and a light was switched on.

Quayle stood with his back to the door smiling at her.

He said: "Well, Sandra . . . I'm glad to see you. You're looking worried but as beautiful as ever."

She said: "Thank you. But I haven't very much time for talking. Miguales will be back by midnight. If I should not be back he might think something. He might be suspicious. . . ."

Quayle said: "Don't let's worry about Miguales for a moment. And you'll be back long before then." He led the way into a room along the narrow passage.

It was a small comfortably furnished room. There was a large desk with two telephones on it. He pushed forward an armchair.

"Sit down and relax, Sandra," he said. He smiled at her cheerfully. She sat down in the chair. She began to feel more confident. He gave her a cigarette; lit it; went to the desk, sat behind it.

He said: "Well . . . ?"

She inhaled the cigarette smoke. She said: "There's very little to tell. Miguales is very careful. He's taking no chances and he's scared—badly scared. He tells me that he has to leave the country within a few days; that the reason for his forced departure is the failure of his mission; that the Government people here don't take him seriously. He professes to be terribly upset about me, because he can't take me with him. He says that he hoped to be able to stay here while the divorce went through so that we could be married. He says that he has practically been *ordered* to leave."

Quayle said shortly: "He's lying. But he can't do anything else. He's in a bad spot. He'll get badly rattled in a little while. Then . . ." He smiled grimly.

She said: "I want to know about Ricky. I'm fearfully worried about him. I think about him all the time."

"Of course," said Quayle. "Of course you think about him all the time. But you needn't worry a great deal, my dear. It could be a damned sight worse for Ricky."

She looked at him. "You mean . . . ?"

"I mean that if we hadn't played it this way Ricky would probably be dead by this time," said Quayle in a matter-of-fact voice. "They'd got him marked down. He was the one person they were certain about. They knew he was the one who dealt with Lelley. That told them what they wanted to know."

"Is he safe now?" she asked.

Quayle shrugged his shoulders. "As safe as any of us are in this game," he said. "But I don't think you have to worry *too* much." He smiled at her. "He's being very well looked after," he went on. "A gentleman—a very tough piece of work indeed—named O'Mara, is looking after Ricky. I expect he'll have something to tell me soon. Then I shall know what I'm doing."

He laughed. "It's going to be damned funny when I tell Ricky the whole story," he went on. "*Very* amusing. It's the first time I've ever had to use the services of a wife in order to make certain of her husband. It's a tough game. By the way, did you get a look at Miguales' passport. I bet it was a diplomatic one?"

She nodded. She asked: "Do you know what you wanted to know. Do you know who . . . ?"

He shook his head. "Not yet," he said. "Let's give O'Mara a chance. O'Mara is the fastest worker I've ever known. He'll start to move in a minute and when he does things will happen."

He lit a cigarette; leaned his elbows on the desk. Looking at him she thought that he radiated a certain confidence; possessed an odd mastery over events and men. She felt better; less frightened.

He said: "Listen, Sandra—you can know this much. Perhaps it will help you to understand. I want you to realise that we haven't played it this way because we don't like Ricky or because we don't trust him. He's done splendid work, but there comes a time when every man begins to weaken a little—especially if he has a temperament like Ricky's. I expected him to slip a little and the only thing I could do was to use the process for my own ends. That's why you had to come into this. But don't worry about it. He'll understand."

He got up. He began to walk about the little room.

He went on: "Some little while ago two of our best agents were killed in Paris. They were picked up originally because of some information secured by the Germans from a woman we employed—a woman called Mavrique.

"They could have got their original information only from one source—Lelley. They knew that when Mavrique was arrested and the other agents killed we, on this side, would know that the information which had enabled them to get our people came from Lelley. But Lelley had lots of time to make a getaway. He'd been back and forth between this country and Eire a dozen times. He could have done it again. But he wasn't going to clear out without orders. He was a tough proposition, was Lelley—a dyed-in-the-wool Nazi. So they left him here. They sacrificed him deliberately."

She said: "I see. They were waiting for you to do something about him. They wanted to see what you would do?"

"Right," said Quayle. "They wanted to see what we would do about Lelley. They knew we knew something about him. They didn't know how much."

Quayle stopped pacing about the room; returned to the desk. He lit a fresh cigarette, inhaled with pleasure.

He went on: "I played into their hands. Years ago Lelley had a woman working over here with him. A very clever piece indeed. They put this woman next to one of my subordinate agents—a man called Stott. Stott fell for her, married her. Probably they had the idea that Stott was important. But she quickly found out that he wasn't; that he was only an underling, doing routine work. So she left him after a few weeks—a business which, I think, has concerned him a great deal ever since." Quayle smiled grimly.

"So Lelley knew about Stott," he continued. "And knowing that, I put Stott in to keep Lelley under observation. I bet they knew all about that too. They would be very pleased with that."

She nodded. "I see," she said. "They could watch Stott."

Quayle said: "They could watch Stott and they could see what we were going to do about Lelley. They weren't particularly interested in Stott. They knew he was small fry. They wanted to see if a bigger fish would be put in to deal with Lelley. We gave them what they wanted. We put in a bigger fish. We put in Ricky . . . and then Lelley had a motor car accident." Quayle sighed.

"Somebody was on to Ricky even before then," he said. "Somebody suspected what Ricky's real job was. Someone who had been sufficiently in touch with him to come to conclusions. When Ricky was telephoned on the night of Mrs. Milton's party they guessed he was going to do something about Lelley. Whoever was keeping an eye on Stott was telephoned and told by this person that Ricky had left town by car. Whoever was watching Stott probably saw the meeting between him and Ricky. Then somebody—with a car—probably one of our friend Miguales' cars—picked Ricky up when he got back to town. After that they had a tail on him all the time. They *knew* now that he was the man they wanted. They were certain."

Quayle drew on his cigarette.

"I pulled a fast one on Ricky," he said, smiling amiably. "I knew that he was a bit nervy; that having pulled off the Lelley job he'd probably let his hair down and have a drink or two. He *does* get a bit nervy sometimes, you know. So I gave him a fake list of our agents in France—just in case.

"Well . . . that one came off. The tail they had on Ricky was a very charming young woman and she managed to get the list off Ricky. But in the process, of course, Ricky got to know her. *He can identify her.* So they've *got* to try and do something about him and they've got to try and do it quickly. That is if they haven't already tried."

Sandra said: "My God . . . they'll kill Ricky . . . they'll kill Ricky. . . ."

Quayle grinned at her. "I wouldn't worry about that," he said. "O'Mara is looking after Ricky. If I had to be looked after by someone *I'd* like it to be O'Mara. He is a *very* efficient one—that one."

She said: "I know you're right. I know you *will* look after him. . . ."

Quayle got up. He said: "You're awfully fond of Ricky, aren't you? One of these fine days I'm going to tell him just how lucky he is." He looked at his wrist-watch.

"On your way, Sandra," he said. "At the end of the street you'll be lucky enough to pick up a taxicab. One of my people will be driving it. Go straight back. And look after Mr. Miguales."

She asked: "What am I to do about him—now?"

Quayle said: "Your attitude now is that you are bitterly disappointed in the way he's played things; that he shouldn't have put you in the position you are now in. That you can't continue to stay at his flat and you can't go back to Ricky. You'd better have a little scene with him and clear out. Go to an hotel. When you're fixed, telephone through to the Overseas Air Conditioning Company in Pall Mall and give the girl your address and telephone number."

"Very well," she said. "I'll do that." She got up.

Quayle went with her to the front door. He said: "You're doing a great job, Sandra. Any time you feel that things are a little tough remember that you're doing it for Ricky as well as for me. Good-night, my dear."

He closed the door quietly behind her; stood, inside the hallway, listening to her receding footsteps.

Then he went back to the little room; sat down at the desk; sat, smoking patiently, waiting for the telephone to ring.

It was nearly eleven o'clock. Therese Martyr and O'Mara sat on high stools at the bar of the Yellow Cantaloupe; drank whisky and soda; regarded the bar and themselves with the satisfaction that comes with a good dinner and pleasant company.

O'Mara was inclined to be talkative. Therese, watching him out of the corner of her eye, thought: He's been away for a long tune. He's glad to be back. He's large, good-natured and possibly a little bit stupid. He *might* be amusing.

He said: "I always knew there'd be trouble in the Kerr *ménage* one day. I wasn't a bit surprised when you told me that the balloon had gone up. Quite obviously that was the sort of marriage that *doesn't* last."

She sipped her whisky and soda. She looked at him over the edge of the glass. She was looking *very* attractive. She knew it.

"Why weren't you surprised?" she asked. "Why was it the sort of marriage that doesn't last?"

O'Mara shrugged his broad shoulders. He said: "The trouble with Ricky is that he's damned temperamental. Clever, mark you, but temperamental. Also he's inclined to be egotistical, and when a man has a wife as beautiful as Sandra Kerr he should try and control his egotism. I expect she was bored with Ricky."

"Possibly," said Therese. "But I think it was something worse than boredom. I think Ricky was rather keen on women in general. I have an idea that there was something on at one time between him and Glynda. Possibly Sandra found *that* out."

"Possibly," said O'Mara with a grin. "Maybe somebody told her."

She smiled at him. O'Mara noted with admiration the beauty of her small, perfectly shaped teeth. She said coolly:

"Glynda was accusing me of that just before you came in. She was quite angry about it. She accused me of making trouble between Ricky and Sandra and then, at the crucial moment, producing the *very* attractive Spaniard—Miguales—with whom Sandra has taken refuge at the moment."

"No!" said O'Mara. "I don't believe it. You wouldn't do a thing like that!"

She was still smiling. She was beginning to find Mr. O'Mara rather attractive. She said:

"No? You'd be surprised. I might easily do such a thing."

He shrugged his shoulders again. He said: "Well . . . I'm damned if I understand women at all. Why should you do a thing like that—unless, of course, you wanted to get your own back on somebody."

She said coolly: "That was Glynda's point. She suggested that I'd been Ricky's mistress and that he'd walked out on me, and so, to even things off, I threw Sandra at Miguales after poisoning her mind against Ricky."

O'Mara laughed. "It won't be so good for you," he said, "if Glynda tells Sandra that. If I know anything of Sandra she'd take a very poor view of you for doing that."

Therese smiled. It was a slow, sweet smile. A rather mechanical sort of smile. She said:

"Should I worry a great deal about that? I don't think I should. Incidentally, Glynda isn't likely to tell Sandra. She daren't. You see, she was a little indiscreet once or twice about Ricky. And she has a very jealous husband. And he has the money. And if someone told him about the Glynda-Ricky episode I don't think it would be quite so good for Glynda. . . ."

"I bet it wouldn't," said O'Mara. "Nice little thing, aren't you, Miss Martyr?" He grinned happily at her. "I think I'd rather be a friend of yours than an enemy. In fact, I'm feeling a little scared of you even now."

He took his cigar-case out of his pocket. It was a dull gold case with his initials, in white gold, in the corner.

She said smilingly: "I don't think that Mr. O'Mara would ever be really scared of a woman. I think you're very experienced, Mr. O'Mara. In fact, I'd even bet that a woman gave you that quite lovely cigar-case."

"Strangely enough you're right," he said. He looked at her sideways. "A lady in Rio gave me the case. It is nice, isn't it?" He handed it to her. She opened it; read the inscription inside—"*To Shaun . . . I shall remember.*" She shut the case with a snap; handed it back.

"I hope she does," she said. Her tone was cynical.

O'Mara sighed. "The trouble with all women is that they never trust each other," he said. "Personally, I think they're right! Another whisky and soda, Miss Martyr?"

She said thank you. "And why not Therese?" she asked. "I feel that we're going to be friends. And I like your name . . . Shaun . . . a charming name. And when I've had my whisky and soda perhaps you'll be very nice and drop me at home—if we can find a cab."

"Of course," he said. "I'd like to do that."

"And then," said Therese slowly. "And then . . . perhaps I can give you a last drink. One for the road."

He grinned at her. "That would be very nice," he said. "I'd like that a lot . . . too . . ."

They finished their drinks. Therese Martyr got off her stool. O'Mara noted with satisfaction the grace with which she moved. He felt that it was impossible not to be interested in Therese.

They moved towards the vestibule.

"Just in case," she said slowly . . . "just in case you should regard me as a very wicked and scheming woman, I think I ought to tell you that the Sandra Kerr-Miguales business isn't going to hurt anybody *too* much."

"No?" said O'Mara. "And why not?"

"Poor Miguales," said Therese. "He's had very bad luck. He came over here on some sort of diplomatic mission—I believe he was trying to put the Franco Government over with the British people—well . . . you can imagine how much chance he had. He's failed. They'll send him back. And he certainly won't take Sandra with him. How can he?"

"I see," said O'Mara. "And what does she do when he's gone?"

She shrugged her shoulders.

"I expect she'll go back to Ricky," she said. "Why shouldn't she? She's very fond of him . . . really . . . Only he *is* so stupid . . . Ah . . . they've actually got a cab for us."

They went outside. In the cab she turned to O'Mara. She said: "Tell me . . . are you the sort of person who kisses women in cabs?"

"Sometimes," said O'Mara. "Only sometimes. It all depends on the woman."

She said: "Of course . . . that was what I was afraid of."

*

O'Mara opened the door of his flat, went inside, switched on the hall light and looked at his wrist-watch. It was just after one.

He went into the sitting-room; threw his hat and overcoat across a chair. He went to the sideboard, poured and drank a small glass of brandy.

He put the glass down; took from the breast pocket of his jacket the note he had taken from the body of the white-faced young man. O'Mara stood in the middle of the sitting-room, smoking one of his small cigars, concentrating on the note. He read it through twice:

"Dear Señor,

"I do not think that you are being very kind to me. I do not think that you are giving me the sort of bargain which we agreed. I have done what I said I would do because I always keep my word, and now when the time comes for you to do your part it seems that I am to be left in the cold. I do not like this. I do not like it at all.

"I hope to find some means of seeing you and of settling this business in an amicable manner. I hope this will be possible. If not, there is only one thing I can do. I should not like to do that because I am a man of honour.

"I hope and expect to hear from you within the next four days. I find myself in the most difficult position.

"E. M."

He put the note back in his pocket. He went to the telephone; dialled a number. After a moment Quayle's voice said: "Hallo!"

O'Mara said: "Peter, can I talk?"

Quayle said: "Yes . . . in a minute. I'll call you back and have the line cut out. Then you can talk."

O'Mara hung up. Two minutes later, Quayle came through. He said: "Go ahead, Shaun . . ."

O'Mara said: "We laid it on at Kerr's flat. They had the place under observation. The usual business. There was a white-faced youngster there. The normal type—tough. He came after me and the Cordover bird after *him*. You know—the old follow-my-leader stuff."

Quayle said softly: "What did you do about that?"

"Just what you think we did," said O'Mara. "At that address you gave me. It worked all right."

Quayle said: "You sound fairly happy, Shaun. Are you getting anywhere?"

"I think I might be," O'Mara replied. "Is there anything additional I ought to know about the Miguales bird?"

"He's getting out," said Quayle. "I heard that to-night. He's scared. If it's possible for a type like Miguales to be scared."

O'Mara smiled. "It can happen," he said. "So he's getting out," he went on. "That's damned funny, Peter."

Quayle asked: "Why is it funny?"

O'Mara said: "Great minds think alike. I've been doing a little funny business with Mrs. Glynda Milton. As a matter of fact she's stooging for me at the moment. She's doing it and liking it because she's got to. For my own purposes I took a chance and told her that Miguales was getting out, and I am very glad to hear that it's true. It makes it a lot easier for me."

There was a pause; then he went on: "Oh . . . by the way . . . this Sandra Kerr business. Why the hell did she have to pick a time like this to go off with Miguales? It's a bit odd, isn't it?"

"No," said Quayle. "It isn't. Not when you come to consider that I told her to do it. She works for me."

"Well, I'll be damned," said O'Mara. "You're a clever old basket, aren't you, Peter?"

"No," said Quayle. "Just intelligent. Like you are."

O'Mara said: "You realise that Ricky's in a spot, don't you? They've got to get Ricky. They've got to get him because he could identify that woman—the one who picked him up in the Green Headdress. So they've got to do that. That is if they've got anybody else now that the white-faced heel is no longer with us. D'you think there's anybody else?"

Quayle said: "I wouldn't know, Shaun."

O'Mara asked: "What about Sandra Kerr and Miguales?"

"She'll be leaving him," said Quayle. "They'll quarrel and she'll leave him. She'll go to a hotel."

There was a pause. Then O'Mara asked: "What am I to do about Miguales? When the time comes, I mean . . . ?"

"Handle it carefully," said Quayle. "It's got to be an accident or something—you know what I mean. He's got a diplomatic passport. That makes things a little difficult."

"Yes . . ." said O'Mara. He went on: "Peter, get me some fingerprints, will you? And get them as quickly as you can."

"Whose?" asked Quayle.

"Magdalen Francis and Elvira Fayle," said O'Mara. "The two women who were at the party."

"All right," said Quayle. "What about Milton and Martyr— the other two?"

"I'm not worrying about them," said O'Mara. "Just get me Francis and Fayle."

Quayle said: "I'll get a man from the Special Branch on the job first thing in the morning. He'll get 'em somehow to-morrow and get them around to your place to-morrow evening. You sound as if you're having a busy time, Shaun."

"Quite busy," said O'Mara. "But it's all good, clean fun. I haven't been so happy for a long time. By the way, you might warn Kerr to stick inside that flat of his for a bit. I don't want anything to happen to him. He's had quite a bit of trouble lately one way and another, hasn't he?"

"Yes," said Quayle. "Incidentally . . . *you* watch your step, Shaun."

O'Mara grinned. "I will," he said. "You'd miss me a lot, wouldn't you . . . !"

Quayle said: "I'd miss the stink of those awful cigars of yours. Well . . . good-night, Shaun."

O'Mara hung up. He stood for a moment looking at the telephone, thinking. Then he re-lit his cigar.

He went to the gramophone; put on a *rhumba* record. He stood in front of the gramophone cabinet, snapping his fingers in time with the music.

CHAPTER THREE
BE NICE TO LADIES

I

O'MARA came out of the Premier Lounge in Albemarle Street, began to walk towards his flat. He had drunk two double whiskies and sodas; felt at peace with the world in general.

It was seven o'clock when he let himself into his flat. He went directly into the sitting-room; saw, on the table, the large sealed packet which Quayle had promised—the report and photographs of the Special Branch man.

O'Mara opened the packet. He ran a practised eye over the pictures, turned to the report, read it. He smiled. All his guesses had been right. He took the packet into the kitchen, extracted one or two items he required, burned the rest.

He went back to the sitting-room; poured himself another drink. He turned on the radio, found a dance band, sat down, glass in hand. He began to think about the woman in Rio . . . wondered if—and when—he should see her again.

He *would* see her again, thought O'Mara. He would see her again because, subconsciously, she existed in his mind; because always when he had a few minutes to spare his conscious thoughts turned towards her. O'Mara considered that such an urge could not possibly be thwarted; that somehow, some time, he would set out for Rio once again, would find her, graceful, gracious, eminently desirable, in her white house with its red roof and attractive shadows. It was essential that all this should happen again. If for no other reason but that history always repeated itself. *If* it were of sufficient importance.

History repeats itself . . . the words, casually thought, brought something to his mind, set a cynical grin about his well-shaped mouth. History might adequately repeat itself, thought O'Mara, and the process might save him a great deal of trouble.

He considered the situation about Lelley. The situation about Lelley, the circumstances of his life, work and death, formed a pattern that was not new in Nazi technique. Lelley had come to an end that was predestined by his own people, his own employers. Lelley had known not enough and too much.

He had been allowed to create and maintain an extensive spy organisation in this country. He had been allowed to do as he liked, given what money he wanted. He had everything except his life. He had lived on the edge of a volcano, where the slightest mistake would mean death. Lelley, who knew this, had probably also realised that his own life was of no importance to the people who employed him. Just as the lives of *his* operatives meant nothing to him. The essence of the Nazi creed was a fanaticism that is not understandable to ordinary minds; a fanaticism of death comparable only to the demoded hara-kiri of the Japanese.

The radio began to play an attractive tune called *I Shall See You Sometime*. O'Mara began to think about the woman in Rio again. Charming and pleasurable scenes flitted through his mind. He began to consider how best business, in that country, could be combined with pleasure. That there was work for him there he was certain. That Quayle would send him back there was also certain. *After* he had finished this job.

O'Mara sighed. The time had come when he must really get down to the business of sweeping up the pieces; of tying the ends. That done, he would think about the lady in Rio. Until then he would determine to forget her.

He finished his drink; went to the telephone, dialled a number. He waited patiently, listening to the music, until the voice of Sammy Cordover came on the line.

O'Mara said: "Good-evening, my bucko, and how are you?"

"Pretty good," said Cordover. "I wondered when you'd be comin' through again."

"Like the poor, I am always with you," said O'Mara pleasantly. "Now listen to me, Sammy. I want you to keep right on the tail of friend Miguales. Stick to him like a sick kitten on a hot brick. You'll probably need help. You can arrange that through our esteemed employer. You'll want to be on watch at his place from now on. Understand? If he leaves, find out where he's going, when he's returning. He's getting ready to leave. Probably he'll be in and out for a bit—packing, settling things up. Keep in close touch with Mr. Q., let him know everything. He'll know where to get me. Have you got that?"

"I've got it," said Cordover. "Anything else?"

"Not at the moment," said O'Mara. "That'll be quite enough to get on with. Good-night!" He hung up.

He began to walk up and down the room. He lit one of his small cigars and gave himself up to the consideration of ways and means. The process took ten minutes. It was a little chancy, thought O'Mara, but not too much so, and when a man is keen on getting back to a place like Rio and . . . Well . . . one chance more or less . . . ?

He went to the telephone, dialled and waited. The voice of the blonde girl, cool and remote, said hello.

He said: "This is O'Mara . . . descendant of *all* the Irish Kings, and don't you forget it. I want to speak to the boss."

He could visualise the blonde girl smiling. She said: "Very well, Mr. O'Mara. Just hold on a minute. He isn't here, but I can arrange a hook up."

"Wonderful," said O'Mara. "What organisation!" He laughed into the telephone. "One of these fine days," he went on, "remind me to tell you a little story about your voice."

"I'd like that, Mr. O'Mara," she said. "I hope it's a nice one."

"A lovely one," said O'Mara promptly. "Nearly as lovely as the voice."

She said demurely: "Please hold on." There was a pause; then Quayle came on the line.

O'Mara said: "Thanks for the pretty pictures and the report, Peter. A quick job."

Quayle asked: "Is it as you thought? Are you satisfied?"

"Very," said O'Mara. "I'm going to get something started. By the way, when all this business is over, can I go back to Rio?"

"Probably," said Quayle. "I take it there is the usual additional reason for your going there. Or do you just like the climate?"

"I like the climate," said O'Mara.

Quayle asked: "When are you going to finish this job off, Shaun? I've an idea that you haven't a great deal of time."

"You're perfectly right," said O'Mara. "I haven't. In fact, I've so little time I'm a trifle scared. You'd be surprised how industrious I'm going to be. Now will you do something for me?"

Quayle said: "Of course."

"I'm going to dine at the Yellow Cantaloupe," said O'Mara. "I've told Cordover to stick to Miguales. He's got to be making a move *very* soon. I've told Cordover to get in touch with you if anything at all happens. Will you—or that girl of yours—call me at the Yellow Cantaloupe. And make it as soon after nine-thirty as you can. I don't want to be stuck there. Is that all right?"

"Yes," said Quayle. "I understand. I take it you're going to do what is usually called 'playing it off the cuff'?"

"Right," said O'Mara. "That's just what I am going to do. I've got to."

"Well . . . good luck to you, and good-night," said Quayle. "And don't stick your chin out *too* far!"

O'Mara hung up. He waited a minute, dialled again. He said softly, in his charming voice:

"Therese . . . my little sweet, I feel very well disposed towards you this evening. And I have the most extraordinary and amazing events to murmur into your shell-like ear. How about dining with me?"

She laughed. She said: "I've an engagement, Shaun—but I'll put it off. You knew I'd do that, of course, didn't you? That's why you've left this invitation until the last moment."

"I hoped you'd come," said O'Mara. "Of course I'm well aware of my fatal attraction *for* lovely women, but even so, thank you for ditching the other fellow."

"It was a woman," said Therese. "But she'll keep. Where shall we dine?"

"Let's go to that place where we met," said O'Mara. "I'm always going to be rather fond of that place. And I like the name—the Yellow Cantaloupe. Will you meet me there at nine o'clock?"

"Very well," she said. "I'll wear my most ravishing frock. I suppose you know that I'm *for* you in rather a big way, Shaun?"

"No?" said O'Mara. "Just fancy that now. And why would that be?"

She said softly: "I'm not quite certain. You're a strange man, and you can be *quite* charming—if you want to—and you've been around, and I like your eyes and your hands. I can't think of anything else, except perhaps that you're one of those damnable people who is always quite certain of himself . . . you take what you want where you want it. You've a nice fresh point of view as well. . . ."

O'Mara said: "You're giving me a swelled head. You make me sound a hell of a guy."

"Which you probably are *not*," said Therese quickly. "Really, I suppose you're quite an ordinary sort of person, but possibly I'm rather fed up with young men with long hair. I think that's it. Just a matter of comparison."

"All right," said O'Mara. "I'll get my hair especially cut for you to-night. *Au revoir*, my love. I'll be seeing you. Incidentally, I think *you're* pretty good. . . ."

"Oh, thank you, my lord," said Therese. "You're awfully kind."

"That's my failing," said O'Mara. "I can't bear to see women suffer. I'm too soft with them."

"Like hell you are," said Therese. "I'll see you at nine."

O'Mara hung up. He began to walk about the room, thinking; working out the details.

Miguales stood in front of the fire, a cocktail glass in one hand, a cigarette in the other. Now that he was alone his features, usually relaxed in a charming smile, were taut. There were hard lines about his mouth. The fingers holding the cigarette twitched nervously.

Miguales put the glass on the mantelpiece; began to walk about the room. He thought to himself that there were definite limits to what one should do; what one should stand for. Brought up as a soldier, Miguales, aware of his flair for attracting people—especially women, had preferred the darker ways of intrigue.

Always he saw himself as the successful secret agent, the individual who by means of brain and charm, could achieve more on the backstairs of war than on the battlefield.

Now he was wondering. Miguales was realising that there was danger in this game. He smiled a little. But he had covered himself very well. The danger was not so great, the chances not so precarious, if you had a diplomatic passport. He had that. He was a Spaniard, entitled to the protection due to a neutral in a belligerent country.

He began to think about Sandra. At the back of his mind was a vague query, almost a suspicion, that he had never quite understood about the Sandra business. He shrugged his shoulders. His mind was made up.

It was with a certain feeling of relief that he began to think about his journey, about his arrival back in his own country. Whatever the situation might be there, it would be better than this. He sighed. Of course if the Sandra Kerr business had been possible it might have been amusing. But it was not possible, and that was that. Miguales, who was a good actor, came to the conclusion that in this scheme he had played his part adequately—if not brilliantly.

He looked at his wrist-watch. It was half-past eight. He went to the bureau in the corner of the room; began to write the note to Sandra.

Outside it was dark. An east wind had sprung up. It was cold. On the other side of the road opposite St. Ervin's Court, Sammy Cordover and Stott stood in the dark recess of a doorway, from which they could observe the entrance of the apartment block opposite. Stott pushed his hands deep into his overcoat pockets.

He said: "This is a hell of a game. Do you like it?"

Cordover moved his head a little. He said: "Why not?"

Stott said: "I often wonder why anybody does this sort of thing. I suppose you do the same sort of work as I do?"

Cordover said: "I wouldn't know. What do you do, Stott?"

The other shrugged his shoulders. "I'm usually a tail for somebody," he said. "I keep places under observation. I watch people. I case places that they want cased. That's about all. It's not a very interesting job, but it gives you time to think. And what's your line?"

Cordover said: "Just about the same as yours. It isn't very exciting, is it?"

On the other side of the road the door opened. The porter came out. He was carrying two large suitcases. A moment later, Miguales emerged. By the light of the half-open door they could see him standing in the entrance whilst the porter went to look for a cab. After a few minutes the man came back. He spoke to Miguales, who shrugged his shoulders.

Cordover said: "He'll probably walk. He's not using his car. He'll have his bags sent on after him, I expect. If he goes I'll take him on. You stay here. You know where to ring me if anybody goes in—anybody you feel I ought to know about."

Stott said: "O.K. I understand."

Miguales said something to the hall-porter, began to walk down the street. When he'd got a little way ahead, Cordover stepped out into the road, went after him. He did not take a great deal of trouble to keep in the shadows. He allowed the man in front to hear his footsteps. Once or twice he thought that Miguales glanced back over his shoulders.

At nine o'clock Sandra Kerr let herself into the Miguales' flat. She went into the sitting-room. The little clock on the mantelpiece struck nine as she entered. She saw the note propped against it. She opened the envelope, read the note:

"My beloved Sandra,

"I am leaving now. I do not think I shall see you again. I know that you will probably come to the flat to see me; that you will expect to find me here; that you will think that I may still have something to say to you. But because I now know that nothing is possible I am going away immediately because I cannot bear to see you again.

"During the last few hours I have made every endeavour, done everything possible, to try and stay in this country. I have been told that I must leave immediately. I shall be leaving by plane early to-morrow morning. There are one or two things that I wish to collect from the flat. I shall be back between ten and eleven. By that time I know you will have gone. I observe that you have done your packing, that everything is ready for you to move.

"Words are of very little avail, Sandra, but you know what is in my heart. I am quite desolate that things could not be otherwise than they are. I shall always remember you. I shall always carry a picture of your beauty in my mind.

"I am, for ever,

"Your devoted,

"Enrico."

She read the note through again, screwed it into a ball with the envelope, threw it into the fire. Miguales, she thought, was very obvious.

She smiled a little. He thought he was a good—such a great—actor, such an intriguer. Really he was indifferent, not very clever, possessed of a certain superficial charm that would delude only an unintelligent woman. She went to the telephone, called Quayle's office. She gave the blonde girl a message to give to Quayle.

II

O'Mara walked into the vestibule of the Yellow Cantaloupe. He saw Therese sitting in the far corner under a shaded light. For a moment O'Mara was concerned with the superb picture which she presented. She was dressed in an aquamarine wool frock, over which she wore a short Persian lamb coat. Her small, beautifully shaped feet were shod with black *glacé* court shoes. She wore no hat and at her throat was a beautiful bar brooch of zircons and diamonds. The colour of the aquamarine frock brought out the green in her eyes.

She got up; came to meet O'Mara. She said: "You see, Shaun, you've practically reduced me to a condition of serfdom. Not only am I here first, but I come to meet you."

O'Mara smiled at her. "I wonder if anybody ever told you that you make a most lovely picture. I was thinking when I came in—"

She interrupted. "What were you thinking?" she asked. Her smile was impertinent.

"I was thinking that I would like to take your nose between my forefinger and thumb, hold it up, and kiss you on the mouth."

She said: "Dear . . . dear . . . dear . . . Mr. O'Mara! And I didn't think you were that sort of man."

O'Mara said: "No?" He cocked one eyebrow.

They went to the bar. O'Mara ordered the drinks.

She asked: "What is all this about, Shaun? I feel there's something in the wind. There is a twinkle in your eye. Something's happened. I want to know what it is. I know it's something exciting."

O'Mara said: "I don't know just how much I can tell you." He looked at her seriously. "In fact," he went on, "I don't know that I can tell you anything. I'm not quite certain if I can trust you, Therese."

She smiled. She said: "Oh no? So you can't trust me. Well, I like that!"

O'Mara said: "I don't care whether you like it or not." He grinned boyishly. "In point of fact," he said, "I've got something very amusing to tell you about the Kerrs. You know, I was intrigued about Ricky Kerr, and I'm a man who loves satisfying his curiosity."

She said: "I see. And so you've satisfied your curiosity about Ricky. And you're going to tell me all about it."

He said: "I'm going to tell you what I think—but not yet. We'll have dinner first."

Therese said: "You intrigue me, Shaun, very much. You're rather mysterious, aren't you? Although I suppose that adds to your attraction."

"Mysterious?" said O'Mara. "Not on your life. I'm the most obvious man that ever happened."

She said: "I wonder. You take a great delight in life and all the good things of life." She looked at him wickedly. "I can't understand how it is that you're not in this war."

He shrugged his shoulders. He said casually: "Maybe I'm a man of peace."

"Like hell you are," said Therese. "I should think you adored killing people."

"That's as maybe," said O'Mara. He drank some whisky and soda. "But killing people is a dangerous game, you know. I like to keep out of trouble. I think the whole essence of life is having a good time without getting too involved in anything."

"I wonder. But perhaps you're right, Shaun. So you're the gentleman who goes about the world having a good time but not getting involved in anything. I suppose in a minute you'll be telling me that you're not involved with me."

O'Mara looked at her sideways. He said: "The impertinence of it. What do you mean—involved with you?" He grinned. "I'm not in so deep that I can't get out," he said.

"Well, I'll be damned!" said Therese. "You've the effrontery to sit on that stool drinking whisky and to tell me that you're not in anything that you can't get out of. You're quite impossible, Shaun."

He leant a little closer to her. He said: "My sweet, listen to me. You're not suggesting that you want me to string along with you for ever, are you? I've got an idea that after, shall we say six months, you might find the process rather boring."

"Not so boring as too exciting," said Therese. "I should want someone to follow you about with a machinegun to keep the other women at bay."

"Why should you think that women find me attractive?" O'Mara asked.

She said: "I don't think, Shaun—I know. You see I'm rather particular about my men. I've fallen for you with rather a bump."

O'Mara said: "Well, one of these fine days you'll have to get up again, won't you? In the meantime—tell me something . . ."

"If I can," she said. She finished her cocktail. "But I want another Martini first of all."

O'Mara ordered the drinks. He said: "This question has something to bear on what I propose to tell you when we've had dinner—this funny little story that I think's going to amuse you so much. Have you known Miguales long? What sort of person is he—this fellow who went off with Sandra Kerr?"

She said: "I don't know him well, but what I do know of him I rather like. I met him five years ago in Biarritz—just before the war. He was doing some diplomatic job for the Spanish Government. He was attractive, attentive and charming. Don't think that there's ever been anything between Enrico Miguales and myself," she said. "I should be annoyed if you thought that. He isn't my type, and in some way he's vaguely stupid."

O'Mara said: "You know, that's funny. I mean your being in Biarritz five years ago. I was over there about the same time. It's amusing to think that we might even have been staying in the same hotel, might even have seen each other."

She said: "Oh no, Shaun. I never saw you."

He raised his eyebrows. "How do you know?" he asked.

She smiled at him slowly. She said, with a sideways look: "If I'd seen you, my dear, at *any* time, I should have done something about it."

They went into the dining-room. O'Mara had reserved a table in the corner. There were some flowers on it; a pink lamp shade. The table was inviting, charming.

He ordered cocktails. He said: "I telephoned through and ordered a special dinner. We've been lucky. This is, apparently, a good day for food at this place. We have hot *hors d'oeuvres*, a chicken and an amazing sweet specially concocted for us. You see what I do for you."

Therese looked at him. Her eyes were glowing. She said: "And what does a girl have to do to be so worthy, Mr. O'Mara?" She smiled at him.

"Drink your cocktail and don't ask leading questions," said O'Mara pertly. He raised his glass. "Here's to you, my sweet."

She said: "I want to hear all about this mysterious business. What is it you have to tell me, Shaun? I'm thrilled. I feel it's going to be exciting. I'm *terribly* impatient."

"I know," said O'Mara. "That's why I kept you such a long time in the bar outside. You could hardly sit still."

"Tell me . . ." said Therese.

O'Mara looked round the room. He said: "This must be kept very quiet. It's damned funny . . . and *not* so damned funny at that when you come to think it out. As I told you, it's about Ricky Kerr. . . ."

She said: "From the first time I met you you've been awfully interested in Ricky. Why? And what's he done now?"

O'Mara said: "You're quite right about my being interested in him. Listen to this one and wonder. Supposing I were to tell you that all this stuff about Kerr being employed in the Ministry of Supply was a lot of nonsense. Supposing I told you that our esteemed Ricky was nothing more nor less than a Secret Service man. What would you say then?"

Therese sipped her cocktail. She said: "I don't know that I'd be awfully surprised. But I *might* be. Is Ricky the sort of person who does a job like that? Isn't he a little too volatile—if you know what I mean."

O'Mara nodded. "I know what you mean," he said. "I'd have thought that too. But still, believe it or not, that's what he is."

Therese said: "Well . . . *nothing* surprises me. Go on, Shaun . . . tell me more."

The page boy from the hall came in. He came to the table. He said: "Mr. O'Mara? There's a call for you. Will you take it?"

"Oh dear," said Therese. "And just as I was beginning to be thrilled. . . ."

O'Mara got up. "Excuse me for one minute," he said. "Anyhow, the story will keep." He smiled at her; went away.

He went into the call-box in the vestibule; closed the door tightly behind him. He picked up the receiver.

Quayle said: "Listen, Shaun . . . ? Right. Sammy Cordover has been through. Our friend has all his arrangements made. He's left his flat some time ago. Sandra arrived after him and picked up a farewell note. He gave her the air as politely as he could. She's gone."

"I see," said O'Mara softly. "And Miguales?"

"He's going back to the flat," said Quayle. "He's going back to pick up some bags and oddments—at ten o'clock. Cordover got that from the porter downstairs. He went after Miguales and left Stott on. Stott's still there."

O'Mara looked at his watch. It was ten minutes to ten. He smiled to himself. The time thing had worked out all right . . . that was something.

He said: "All right, Peter. I'm going round to see our friend. I'll tell Stott to lay off. We don't need him any more. I'll be seeing you."

He hung up.

He went slowly back to the dining-room. The waiter was beginning to serve dinner.

Therese said: "Ah . . . so you're returned to me. This food is wonderful."

O'Mara looked sorrowful. He said: "Listen, sweet . . . I've got to go. I don't *want* to. I've *got* to. That was my boss talking just now. Believe it or not he wants me to go to Ireland first thing in the morning on Supply business. I don't want to. I want to stay right here for a bit." He smiled at her. "So I'm going off immediately to try and talk him out of it."

She said: "Oh dear . . . how annoying. *Must* you go, Shaun? What about your dinner? And what about *me*?" She made a little *moue* of annoyance.

"I don't mind missing my dinner," said O'Mara. "It's you I'm worrying about. But I must go. I must try and talk him out of this . . . for both our sakes."

She asked: "How long will you be?"

He shrugged his shoulders. "Perhaps an hour—perhaps more."

She said with a little smile: "Well . . . if you have to go to Ireland perhaps you can take me. That *would* be nice. But to be serious . . . if you must go you must. When you've finished come back to the flat. I'll be waiting for you. I consider I can cook the best omelette in England. With *real* eggs. I'll do it for you myself." She dropped her eyes. "I gave my maid a night off to-night."

O'Mara smiled at her. He said: "You're quite wonderful, Therese. Let's do that. I'll fix about the bill here outside; get

this interview over as soon as I can and rejoin you at the flat."
He paused for a moment; then went on: "You didn't really
mean that thing about Ireland, did you?"

She raised her eyebrows. "Why not, silly?" she asked. "If
you can get the exit permit."

O'Mara said: "Well . . . I'll be damned. What a woman it is!
Well . . . *au revoir*. I'll see you at the flat. Eat a good dinner."

She said: "I will. But all the time I shall think about you."

"What a subject for thought," said O'Mara.

He smiled down at her. He went away.

Sandra hesitated on the threshold; then inserted her key
in the lock, pushed open the door. She could see the light in
the sitting-room. She crossed the hallway, pushed open the
sitting-room door, closed it behind her, stood with her back
against it.

Ricky Kerr got up from the desk on the other side of the
room. He smiled at her. He came towards her. He said:

"Well, Sandra, so you've come back—or have you?"

They stood looking at each other; then suddenly they both
began to laugh. They stood a few feet from each other in the
centre of the sitting-room laughing.

Eventually she said: "Yes, I've come back, Ricky. You've
been very wicked, haven't you?"

He took her in his arms. "I know all about it, my dear—
all about it. If it's possible for a person like myself to learn a
lesson, I've learned it."

She put her finger on his mouth. She said: "I know—and
it's going to be much easier from now on, isn't it? You see, you
won't have to pretend any more."

Kerr said: "Not now. Quayle's been on the telephone to
me this evening. He's told me the whole bag of tricks. You're
a fine one, aren't you?" He looked at her. There was admiration in his eyes.

She asked: "Do you really mean that, Ricky?"

Kerr said: "What do you think? *I* think you're the loveli-est—most wonderful—thing in the world. I know that and I'm not going to take any more chances on you."

She said: "No? Not with such lovely people as Elvira, and Magdalen and Glynda and Therese?"

"Not even for people like that," he said. "Anyway, they're not even in your street." His face became serious. "I've learned another sort of lesson too," he went on, "and that is not to take any more chances—as far as Quayle is concerned, I mean. He's taught me a hell of a lesson—that one."

Sandra said: "You mean he's made use of you. Made use of a lapse on your part. Well, Ricky . . . even if you have been a stooge you've been a very useful one. Incidentally, I've been little more than a stooge myself."

"Some stooge," said Kerr. He kissed her again.

She said: "I need a drink and I'm going to give you one. I've been rather scared the last few days."

Kerr said: "I bet you have. So have I. Sticking around here hasn't been too good, I can tell you. I felt very impatient at times. Tell me something. . . ."

She said: "You needn't worry, Ricky. My *affaire*—if it can be called an *affaire*—with Señor Miguales was most platonic." She laughed. "I don't think he ever wanted it to be anything else. I think he was rather scared of me."

"You're telling me," said Kerr. "You scare me too, some-times."

She said over her shoulder: "That's as it should be." She poured out the drinks. When she brought his drink to him, she said nervously:

"Ricky, what's going to happen?"

He shook his head. He said: "I don't know. Quayle wants me to stay here. Maybe he'll find a use for me. But there's a person called O'Mara running this thing at the moment, and you can take it from me he's *some* man. He's dynamite. I'd rather be his friend than his enemy."

Sandra said in a low voice: "What will they do?"

Kerr shrugged his shoulders. "I don't know. One thing's obvious. O'Mara's got to make a clean-up. He must. He daren't let any of these people get away with it. He daren't let any of them. . . . God knows what he's going to do about it. It's a tough proposition."

He lifted his glass. He said: "Well, here's to you, my sweet. And here's to O'Mara. Good luck to him."

They drank the toast together.

Miguales stood in front of the fireplace smoking a cigarette. For the first time for some days he felt peaceful and contented. At long last he could see his way before him. He felt he had come out of a valley of fear and indecision; that the road was now clear. In twenty-four hours he would be away from this accursed country with its dark and its cold and its rain—with its ominous shadows. He began to congratulate himself. Of course you had to be a little tough now and then. You had to play things along. You had to act. You had to use your brains. Miguales thought he had done all these things and even if his employers were hard people, well, he had been smart enough for them.

He lit a cigarette; went to the sideboard. He examined the cocktail shaker. There was still some Martini in it. He poured out a glass; went back to the fire.

Outside in the street it was dark. O'Mara came slowly down on the side opposite the apartment block. He found Stott standing in a doorway leaning against the wall, his hands in his pockets, deep in thought.

O'Mara said: "You're Stott, aren't you?"

Stott said: "Yes. You're Mr. O'Mara?"

O'Mara said: "That's right. Has anything happened?"

Stott said: "No. He's still inside. He's not leaving till the morning."

O'Mara said: "Right. Well, you're through, Stott. You can go home and smoke your pipe or make yourself a pot of tea, or do any of the things you do when you're at home."

Stott smiled in the darkness. He said: "Thanks, Mr. O'Mara." He went quietly away.

O'Mara stood in the shelter of the doorway. He lit one of his small cigars. He put his hand inside the breast of his jacket, felt the butt of the Luger pistol in his inside pocket. He walked across the road.

Inside the hallway of St. Ervins Court the hall-porter sat in his little office immersed in the evening paper.

O'Mara said: "Mr. Miguales? I hear he's not leaving till the morning. He's expecting me."

The porter said: "His flat's on the first floor. Shall I take you up?"

O'Mara shook his head. "Don't bother," he said. "I'll walk up the stairs. The exercise is good for me."

Miguales was drinking his second Martini when he heard the key in the lock. He was not surprised. He thought that would be the porter. His eyes opened a little when the door opened and O'Mara came in.

O'Mara stood in the doorway smoking his cigar, the Luger pistol in his right hand hanging down by his side.

He said: "Good-evening, Señor Miguales. How do you do? I'm glad to meet you."

He stood quite still, smiling amiably.

Miguales said: "I don't understand—"

O'Mara said shortly: "You will. Just sit down, Miguales. You and I have something to discuss."

Miguales said: "I insist on knowing who are you. Are you from the police? I have a right to know who you are. I should like you to know that I have a diplomatic passport."

O'Mara grinned. He raised the Luger pistol a few inches.

He said: "I have yet to learn that a diplomatic passport would be of any use to you against this. But if you want to know who I am, I'll satisfy your curiosity. My name's O'Mara. I'm one of those people whom you and your friends don't like very much."

He moved into the room. He went on: "I think it's a little tough on you, Miguales. You've got everything nicely sewn up. I imagine that you've been paid your thirty pieces of silver and now all you have to do is to get out. That's right, isn't it? You take a plane some time to-morrow, you flash your diplomatic passport and then you are home. You are at home and you can recount your adventures to your friends; tell them how clever you've been; what fools the English are; and what fools your employers are. I think you're a very clever person, Miguales. The trouble is you're not clever enough. Not by a hell of a long way."

Miguales was about to speak. He stopped for a reason which he could not understand. He stopped as O'Mara came into the centre of the room. Possibly the reason that he did not talk was because he saw the look on O'Mara's face.

O'Mara said shortly: "Sit down. Listen. I've got a good idea of you, Miguales. You're a man of straw—an air balloon. It was only right and proper that the people who've been using you—those charming people for whom you've been working—should have used you as a stooge. I should like you to know that I have very little use for people like you."

Miguales said: "I don't understand what this is. You come here. You have a pistol. You threaten me. Well . . ." He squared his shoulders. "Supposing you kill me, what good do you do? I'm a Spanish citizen—a neutral. My Government expect me to return. You will create a situation between our countries." He stopped talking because he saw that O'Mara was laughing.

O'Mara put the pistol in his pocket. He said: "All right. I won't threaten you. I've got something better than that. Sit down and listen to me."

Miguales said: "I am prepared to listen. I'm quite reasonable."

He was thinking quickly; trying to arrive at a conclusion. What was this? Miguales' mind raced as he endeavoured to come to some logical explanation. But he could find no answer. All he could do was to play for time.

He repeated: "I am quite reasonable."

"You'll be reasonable," said O'Mara. "You'll be reasonable because I'm not demanding much of you—not very much. I'm going to ask you a question and you're going to answer it. Exactly what happens to you depends on how you answer that question, but I haven't a lot of time to waste on you, Miguales," O'Mara went on with his charming smile. "I ought to warn you about that."

Miguales sat back in the big armchair, his hands on its arms. He had a peculiar cold sensation in the pit of his stomach. He was afraid of O'Mara.

O'Mara said: "A few nights ago a German agent called Lelley had an accident at Nelswood. An individual who was concerned in that accident—a man by the name of Kerr, whose wife you know—returned to London. Someone picked him up—followed him—on the way back—someone who could drive a car at night even with the present restrictions. Possibly"—said O'Mara with a cynical grin—"a car with Diplomatic Corps plate on it.

"In any event," he continued, "somebody picked up Kerr. And he was followed. You and your friends kept a tail on him for some time. Then fate was rather kind to you. The following day Kerr was given a list of British Agents in France. That evening he picked up a girl—a rather attractive girl, I imagine—in a public house called the Green Headdress. He went home with her. Early in the morning she stole the list. She disappeared. You understand all that?"

Miguales said: "I understand what you say. But I do not see what it has to do with me. I do not understand why I should be interested in your friend Kerr. It is true that there was something between his wife and me. But that is finished. I know nothing of him. I—"

"All right," interrupted O'Mara. "Now who was the woman and where is she now?"

There was a pause; then Miguales said softly: "Señor, I assure you . . ."

O'Mara said: "Don't give me anything like that. Don't tell me one of your fancy stories, Miguales. You're going to tell me who that woman was. You're going to tell me where she is. Make up your mind about that. Now I'm going to give you a very good reason why you will tell me. Would you like to hear it?"

Miguales said: "Señor, I'm prepared to listen to anything. I do not of necessity know what you're talking about."

O'Mara said: "All right. Well, you listen to this. When your lady friend got that list from Kerr that was very nice for you—but not quite so good as you thought, because the list was a fake one. You see," said O'Mara sardonically, "we aren't such fools as you think—not quite. But there was something else that had to be dealt with. Ricky Kerr had to be dealt with. It was very necessary that the people who employ you and the lady that Kerr met at the Green Headdress should get him out of the way, because he'd seen that girl. He could recognise her. So Kerr had to be removed."

O'Mara drew on his cigar with pleasure. He got up, began to walk about the room.

He said: "That was quite a simple business. There was a white-faced young man employed by the organisation, who was put in to keep observation on Kerr's flat. His business was first of all to see if anyone called on Kerr. The second thing was in due course to remove Kerr. Mrs. Kerr was got out of the way—quite cleverly, I must say"—said O'Mara—"by your good self.

"Now," O'Mara went on, leaning against the sideboard, regarding Miguales with an almost benevolent look, "the plot thickens—as they used to say in the story books. It seems that you wrote a letter to your employer. You weren't very keen on your employer. You hadn't had a straight deal, had you? You wanted to get out, Miguales, because you were getting frightened. So you wrote that letter and you addressed it to dear Señor somebody or other. You had that letter delivered and it was received by the person you intended to receive it. That person was your employer."

O'Mara paused and inhaled cigar smoke. Then he went on: "Writing that letter was a very foolish thing, Miguales. If you had any sense you'd have realised that you knew a little too much. That the people who'd been glad to make use of your services in this country—services which were doubly useful because you had an excellent background and also certain diplomatic privileges—weren't going to stand any nonsense from you. That letter showed them that you were getting a little out of hand; that you were going to finish; that you wanted to be paid off and done with the business. So they had to arrange something for you. Do you know what they planned for you? Would you like to know?"

Miguales said nothing. He sat, turned sideways in the chair, his eyes on O'Mara's. His face was set.

"This is what they planned for you," said O'Mara. "Exactly the same thing as they did to Lelley. They made a stooge out of Lelley. They let him work here for years. They left him here to die just so that they could get a line on us or one of us. In your case the technique was to be a little different. I'll tell you what it was. Your employer took the letter which you had written and rubbed out the name so that the letter began: 'Dear Señor—' That letter was put in an envelope and planted in the inside pocket of the white-faced young man who was keeping observation on Kerr's flat. You understand why, don't you, Miguales?"

Miguales said slowly: "No . . . no . . ."

"Well, I'll tell you," said O'Mara. "Don't you see, you poor fool, the person who employed you knew perfectly well that we should keep Kerr's flat under observation, and that we should get on to that white-faced young man; that if he were picked up or arrested, that letter incriminating you would be found in his pocket. Don't you understand that? It wouldn't have been so bad if this young gentleman had been picked up or arrested; there still might have been an out for you. You might have been able to evolve some sort of story—some explanation. But he wasn't picked up or arrested. Do you know what happened?"

Once again Miguales said: "No . . ." His hands were trembling a little.

"The body of that young man was found in an empty house," O'Mara went on. "He'd been killed—shot. Your letter was found on him. That letter was a letter of complaint that you hadn't had a square deal; that you were going to do something about it." O'Mara grinned. "You see, history repeats itself, my friend," he said. "The story is that you killed that young man. You killed that young man because there had been some quarrel, some difference, between you two, both of whom had worked for Lelley and Lelley's boss. Now your diplomatic passport might possibly protect you against espionage, but you'll find it won't protect you against a murder charge—not in these days. You killed that man. You killed him because he knew too much about you. You killed him because some agreement made between you two had been broken."

Miguales said hoarsely: "That is a lie . . . that is a lie . . . ! I have never killed anyone."

O'Mara said pleasantly: "*I* believe you. I don't think you've got enough guts to kill anyone. You'd do it by proxy. But it's a good lie. It's going to stop you leaving this country. It's going to put you in a Court, it's going to try you for murder, and if I know anything about it, it's going to hang you by the neck until you are dead. And how do you like that, Señor Miguales?"

Miguales said in a thick voice: "This is a trick . . . a dirty despicable trick. This is a trap . . ."

O'Mara yawned. He said: "That's what I am trying to point out. This was a trap set for you by the person for whom you work—the person for whom Lelley worked. The technique, you notice, is always the same. Lelley did his job of work. He was left here to be disposed of. You've done your job of work—you're to be dealt with. The white-faced young man did his job of work and he got his. Quite a dry-cleaning organisation, isn't it?"

Miguales said: "I don't know anything about the killing of that man. How do I know that you are not bluffing? How do I know that the man is dead? I have only your word. I do not want to believe that he is dead."

"Of course you don't," said O'Mara amiably. "But the fact remains he is dead. I ought to know. *I* shot him. So I'm certain about that. The point is that there's an excellent case against you. Because that letter was found on him. Because you and he—according to that letter—had fallen out."

O'Mara grinned happily. "Naturally," he continued, "you will say that the letter was not written to the white-faced young man; that it was written to someone else. Well . . . if that's your case then you're going to find yourself, still, in a very difficult position. If you didn't write the letter to that fellow *tell me to whom you did write it*. I don't think you'll do that. Scared as you are, you haven't the nerve to do that."

Miguales said nothing. There were little beads of sweat on his forehead.

"So their story is," continued O'Mara, "that there was a connection between you and the young man who was put in to watch Kerr—to kill Kerr. The young man whom we know worked for a Nazi organisation in this country. You quarrelled with him. You wrote him that note. He refused to meet your demands and so you killed him. Well . . . it isn't very nice for you, is it?"

There was a silence; then Miguales said: "It seems that I am in a very difficult position. As a man of honour . . ."

O'Mara said: "Don't make me laugh. You're not a man of honour. Listen, you're leaving to-morrow by plane, aren't you? Your passport's in order. Your permit's in order. Well, there's no reason why you shouldn't leave. In point of fact you will leave. You'll leave because I'm going to let you leave. I want you to go, Miguales. *I* don't want you to stay here and die. But there's only one way you'll achieve the business of leaving this country. I want the name and the whereabouts of the girl who picked up Kerr in the Green Headdress."

Miguales got up. He stood, his back to the fire, looking at O'Mara. He said: "Supposing for the sake of argument that by some means I could give you this information . . . supposing I could . . . would you give me your word that I shall be permitted to leave?"

O'Mara said: "Have a heart. What's the good of talking like that, Miguales? It's theatrical. What's the good of my giving you my word or anything else? You're taking a chance on it. You know who I am. You can guess who I work for. I work for the people who dealt with your friend Mr. Lelley. I tell you this—give me the information I want about that girl and so far as I'm concerned you can have your trip to-morrow and I hope you'll enjoy it. But make up your mind quickly."

Miguales said: "My mind is made up. I have been treated with contumely and contempt. I have not been treated by these people as a man of honour. I shall tell you who the girl is. I shall give you her address."

He walked to the bureau in the corner of the room. He took a piece of paper and a pencil. He wrote down the name and address. He gave it to O'Mara.

O'Mara looked at the piece of paper. He folded it, put it in his pocket. He said: "I think you are a very wise man, Miguales. *Adios, Señor.*"

O'Mara closed the door softly behind him.

Miguales stood looking at the blank wall in front of him. He said to himself: "*Madre de Dios*, the escapes you have, Enrico . . . the escapes you have."

Outside O'Mara, his hands in his pockets, walked slowly down the street. He considered that the interview with Miguales had been eminently successful—as successful as he had hoped it would be.

He walked for a little way until he found at the intersection at the two main streets a telephone box. He went inside; dialled a number.

He said: "Quayle? . . . Oh, Peter, I'm having quite a nice evening. An interrupted dinner—but everything else seems to be turning over quite nicely. By the way, you remember that Green Headdress lady? Her name is Esmeralda Valoz. She lives at 117 Thorpe Court, Bayswater. I thought you'd like to know."

Quayle said: "I like to know very much. Nice work, Shaun."

O'Mara said: "Look . . . just a little idea of mine . . . don't do anything about the lady until I call you again. It might not be politic."

Quayle said: "You should know, Shaun. I'll do nothing before I hear from you."

O'Mara said: "That suits me very well. Good-night, Peter."

He hung up the receiver. He went out of the telephone box, looked at his watch. He sighed; began to walk slowly into the darkness.

III

O'Mara stood in front of the radiogram, listening to a new *rhumba* record. He had a glass of whisky and soda in one hand, the stub of one of his little cigars in the other. He was unhappy in so far as such a process was possible to an individual of his characteristics and nature.

He was unhappy because of the music of the *rhumba* which touched a responsive chord somewhere in his being; produced a nostalgia for those places, those people who lived and loved with the music of the *tango*, the *rhumba*, the *maxixe*.

O'Mara who concealed and controlled a temperament as tempestuous as it was artistic, longed, he believed, for the hot pavements, the atmosphere, the odours of South America. For the horses, the women, the nights; for all those sights and sounds which rounded off his life in that place and made for what seemed to him now complete happiness.

He was, in fact, rather like the tragedian who wishes to be a comedian. He had a flair for not appreciating his own peculiar abilities. Abilities that suited and aided his career; that made him a superb employee at the nerve-racking job that was his.

O'Mara, who enjoyed his profession because it brought adventure and colour into his life, would, had he been permanently employed in the Argentine, have longed for the sounds and sights of London. Always, to him, the women who were, at the moment, unattainable were doubly attractive. Because he was in London the lady in Rio was eminently desirable. Had he been in Rio she would—as she had before—have had good cause to worry over his infidelity.

It was this streak in his nature which, at the moment, produced the feeling of dissatisfaction. His flat, although new to him, gave him a feeling of well-being and satisfaction. He felt he would like to stay in it, listening to Argentine music, drinking quietly by himself.

The idea of the night's work before him gave him little pleasure. It was a job. It was necessary. It must be done, and as successfully, in as *finished* a manner, as possible. For in his own manner O'Mara was an artist.

The little patent clock on a side table, an inanimate witness of many peculiar scenes in O'Mara's life, struck a single note. He looked at it. It was half an hour after midnight. He went into the bedroom, took off his velvet dressing-gown, put on his double-breasted coat, examined the Luger pistol, replaced it in the inside pocket, prepared to go out.

O'Mara smiled a little cynically. He was thinking of the innumerable times, in innumerable places, when he had prepared to go out; adjusted his tie, set his soft hat at its jaunty angle; felt, beneath his left armpit, the weight of the bulbous-nosed Luger pistol. This was a scene which he had enacted so many times that he was inclined to associate it with something akin to boredom. For himself—not for others. For that same preparation for departure had, often, spelled death for quite a few people whose end, at the apt hands of Mr. O'Mara, had been artistic if somewhat violent.

One day, he thought, he would go out and, possibly, would not return. One day, no doubt, someone would be a little more clever, a little quicker than himself.

He sighed, looked round the sitting-room, turned off the light, closed the front door of the flat quietly behind him.

Walking, not too quickly, towards Therese's flat, he thought about Miguales. The world was filled with people like Miguales, O'Mara considered. They almost grew on trees. They were clever people; egotists; people with an overdeveloped sense of their own abilities, their own instincts; their own intuitions. They were fair game for the really clever ones of the world, the fanatics, the really tough, dyed-in-the-wool, Nazi type that took no heed of life or death if it could achieve the will of the Fuehrer. Vaguely, cynically, O'Mara felt a little sorry for Miguales. Anyhow, the thought was a sentimental one, thought O'Mara—who liked to consider himself a sentimentalist—and in any event it cost nothing.

It was one o'clock when he arrived at the flat. He rang the bell once, stood waiting patiently, his soft hat in his hand, thinking about Therese, being glad that, at least she had found sufficient attraction in him, his manner and personality, to allow the processes that were slowly working themselves out to be possible.

She opened the door. She stood, smiling at him, the door held wide. He looked at her appreciatively. She wore a long corded velvet house-coat in a peculiar shade of cerise—almost matching her lipstick; her small feet were shod in *mules* of the same colour. The buttons down the front of the house-coat were in antique silver and there was a wide sash of velvet, of the same shade as the coat, but in a plain pattern, about her waist.

O'Mara said: "You look good enough to eat. And I could eat you!" His voice sounded a little thick.

She said: "Gallantly spoken, Mr. O'Mara. But you will probably prefer the omelette. Come in."

O'Mara stepped into the long hallway. He turned towards her as she closed the door, took her in his arms.

She kissed him passionately. She said: "You are an appalling, unfaithful, person. I wouldn't trust you further than I could see you. But you've got something. Definitely . . . Shaun."

She released herself from his arms. "I hope your interview with your chief was successful?" she queried. "I hope he's going to let you do what you want to do."

O'Mara followed her into the drawing-room. It was a long delightful room. The walls were of pale green, the brocade curtains of a deeper shade; the furniture covered with a dark green velvet. A fire glowed in the grate. By its side a small table was set for O'Mara's supper.

He said: "Well . . . he's not. He's being tough and I've got to go to Eire in the morning whether I like it or not. That isn't so good. The idea of taking a plane at nine o'clock doesn't appeal to my aesthetic sense." He shrugged his shoulders.

"Believe it or not," he went on, "I'd like a drink. A great deal of whisky, my sweet. Is that possible?"

"Everything is possible," she said. She poured out the drink, a very strong one, splashed in some soda, brought it to him.

He stood in front of the fire. He was swaying a little; just a little.

She thought: He's fed up. He's annoyed at having to go. So he's drunk a little too much.

"But everything has its advantages," said O'Mara. "You see, my chief, as you call him, is rather fond of me. I was a little bit tough about this Eire job. So he's trying to make it as easy as he can for me."

"Yes?" said Therese. She stood close to him, looking at him, smiling. "Tell me," she said.

O'Mara took a big gulp of whisky. He coughed a little. Then he finished the whisky in one swallow; handed her the glass.

"Believe it or not," he went on, "believe it or not, my sweet, he said that if I wanted to take you with me for a week or so that was all right by him. . . ."

Therese pursed up her pretty lips. She looked at him sideways. She said: "Shaun! Is it true? May I really go with you? You're not teasing me?"

O'Mara held open his arms. She wriggled into them.

He said: "I'm not kidding, Therese. You definitely can come. I could have had your exit permit to-night if I'd wanted it. My boss is quite a *big* fellow, you know. He *can* do things. But that's a detail. I can get the permit any time. We'll have a hell of a time. You'll come?"

She laughed. A little tinkling laugh. She said: "Of course. You're quite marvellous, Shaun. And I'm going to give you another drink and have one myself to celebrate."

She mixed the drinks. When they had finished them, she said: "I wonder why I go for you like I do. I'm behaving like an inexperienced young woman. And I'm certainly not *that*!"

O'Mara said: "You're telling me!" He kissed her.

After a minute she disengaged herself from his arms.

"I'm going to make your omelette," she said. "You need food. You've been drinking a little too much. Then when you've had it I want to hear all about this trip of ours, and then you'll have to go. If I am to be ready for you early in the morning you certainly must go *soon*."

"Directly I've eaten the omelette," said O'Mara, "I'll go."

"No," said Therese. "Not directly. First of all I want to hear about Ricky. My curiosity is unsatisfied. And I'm a woman. I've got to hear all about Ricky and the mysterious secret service business."

"I'll tell you," said O'Mara. He helped himself to some whisky. "I'll tell you all about it when I've had my omelette. I'm in a mood to-night when I could tell you all sorts of things."

She smiled at him. Looking at her, O'Mara thought that she was one of the most attractive women he had ever seen in his life; that she possessed something, some strange quality, independent of looks or colouring, that made her beautiful; that imbued her with a peculiar charm that was entirely her own.

She said: "So you could tell me all sorts of things. Shaun, that either means that you trust me or that you are a victim of the God alcohol which opens all men's mouths. I wonder which it is."

O'Mara grinned at her. "If I didn't trust you," he said, "I shouldn't drink so much when you're around. So the answer is that I *do* trust you. I'd like to tell you about that. Come here."

"No," said Therese, "I will not. Not until you've had that omelette."

"I doubt if you could make one to my liking," said O'Mara, "I'm very particular about omelettes."

"I'll show you about that," she said. She went away. In a minute O'Mara could hear her in the kitchen. He imagined her deft hands, her quick fingers, her graceful movements as she worked. A hell of a woman, thought O'Mara. A hell of a woman. . . .

When she came back with the omelette O'Mara was lounging in the big armchair, his long legs stretched out towards the fire. He looked at her sleepily. He said:

"You know, Therese, if I were the sort of man who considered seriously falling in love with someone I think I'd do it with you. And what do you know about that?"

Therese put the dish on the small table, moved it towards him.

She said: "I'd sooner be permanently associated with a crocodile. You're the most delightful man, Shaun, and taken in small doses, I'm sure you'll prove unique. But to be with you permanently . . . ! My dear man, *any* woman would bore you after six months merely because there wouldn't be anything new for you to find out about her; merely because you'd know all the answers. Eat your omelette. Anyhow, I can cook!"

O'Mara said: "I wonder if *any* man—no matter how long he lived with you, could ever find out all the answers. I think you're a mysterious woman. Your breasts are a little flat, but beyond that you're dynamite. And that's what *I* think."

"Dear me," said Therese. "How very odd. Would you mind eating your supper before you begin to analyse any other physical defect that has come to your notice."

He laughed at her. "Why not?" he asked. "Anyhow, I prefer eating. . . ."

She looked at him sideways. "You're the type who would like to have your cake and eat it too . . . wouldn't you?" she asked.

O'Mara said nothing. He began to eat his supper. She sat on a little stool with a velvet cushion on it and watched him.

It was half-past two. O'Mara had drawn the big settee up in front of the fire. He lay back, his head propped against the cushions. Therese lay in his arms.

She said softly: "I'm an awful fool about you. I've known you for such a little while. I find myself doing everything you want; trying to be what you want me to be. And now I'm going to do the ultimately foolish thing. I'm going to Eire with you." She sighed. "I wonder what happens to a woman who goes to a place like Eire with a man like Mr. O'Mara," she said.

O'Mara grinned. He said: "She has a hell of a good time, and when it's all over she comes back to England and forgets all about it. That is, if she's as wise a woman as I think she is."

Therese said: "I'm wise enough, Shaun. But I wonder if there's enough wisdom in the world for a woman to deal with a man like you." She made a face at him, put up her mouth to be kissed. The kiss took a long time.

Then she said: "Tell me about Ricky. I'm beginning to feel a little sorry for Ricky. I'm beginning to feel that although my intentions were of the best I shouldn't have allowed Sandra to meet Miguales. I should have *known* there'd be trouble."

O'Mara said: "You should worry about Ricky. He ought to be able to manage his own affairs. Ricky's been a damned fool. To have a job as important as the one he had, to have the security of his country, and its interests, in his hands, and then to fall down on the job just because he has to drink too much, and because he can't resist a woman—*any* pretty woman. . . . Ricky makes me tired."

There was a silence. Then she said: "But, Shaun, you ought to make allowances. If Ricky was really doing secret service work—if he was doing dangerous work like that—he's entitled to consideration—even yours."

"Why?" asked O'Mara brusquely. "Why should I consider him? I'm doing the same job myself. I've taken twenty chances for every one that Ricky's taken. But I don't make a damned fool of myself."

She said: "My God! Is that true, Shaun? D'you mean that you too are . . ."

"Yes," said O'Mara with a grin. "I've been doing *that* sort of work for years. Now, when I arrive back in England I have to set to work and try to clear up the mess that damned fool's made of things. Anyhow, I've done *that*. That's something." He smiled into her eyes. "And anyway I've got Eire as a reward."

She said: "I might have guessed. I might have guessed that a man who can suddenly arrange to fly to Eire at an hour or so's notice, and take a doting woman with him, *must* have some sort of pull. So that's the story. Well . . . now you've told me, quite obviously you're *that* sort of man. It's lovely of you to trust me, Shaun."

O'Mara said: "Goddam it! I've got to trust *somebody*. And I trust you. I tell you this thing's been getting me down. I've worried myself sick about it. I haven't known what the hell to do; where to start. Still . . . it's all right . . . that's why we can go to Eire. As usual my luck held. I had a lucky break and everything's going to be all right. I *hope*."

She snuggled closer to him. She said: "Shaun, darling Shaun . . . tell me about the poor foolish Ricky. . . ."

O'Mara said: "Give me another drink, honey, and I'll give you the whole works. Although it's a hell of a long story."

She got up; got the drink; brought it to him. Then she sat down on the rug, leaning against the edge of the settee, looking into the fire. She was thinking that O'Mara was like all men; that it doesn't matter how big or strong a man might be, always there is some breaking point in his mind where he *has* to talk. Every man was like that. The best and the worst. She put her hand over O'Mara's big fingers, squeezed them.

O'Mara finished the whisky. He reached down with his free hand, put the glass on the floor. He said:

"The Nazis had a fellow—an agent—over here working for them. A pretty clever sort of card. A man named Lelley. Lelley had been here for years. He played the part of a country squire at a place called Nelswood. He'd dug himself in well, complete with background and everything. His main job was to get information out of the country and, as you can guess, that isn't an easy thing to do in war-time."

Therese said softly: "I should have thought it an impossible thing."

"So should I," said O'Mara. "But Lelley did it. He worked it all sorts of ways but especially in one way—through a group of German agents in Eire. See?"

"I see," she said. "So *that's* why we're going to Eire?"

"Right," said O'Mara. "Maybe I'm going to do a little cleaning up there. You'll be a great help. You can act as the scenery—the background. Mrs. O'Mara, in fact."

"You've got a supreme nerve—the way you take me for granted!" said Therese. "But tell me more about the mysterious Lelley."

"Lelley was doing fine," O'Mara went on. "Our people knew about him and they were giving him his head. They wanted to see just what he'd do next. Well . . . he did it. He got information over to the enemy that caused the death of some of our best agents, so it was agreed that it was time that Lelley was removed. Well . . . that was easy . . . but there was an interesting string attached to the business. Are you interested, my sweet?"

"I'm thrilled," said Therese. "You're making me feel awfully important, Shaun. Go on. What was the interesting string?"

O'Mara said: "After Lelley had got the information away there was plenty of time for him to make a getaway. But he didn't. He stayed put. Although he must have known that the last job *must* have given him away, he stayed put. Well . . . there was only one reason for that. The people who employed Lelley wanted to see what was going to happen. They wanted to find out just what we would do about Lelley. They knew that if we dealt with him we should think we'd got rid of a damned nuisance and might possibly slacken off and take things a bit easier."

Therese asked: "Whom do you mean by 'they'—the people in Germany who employed Lelley—the Nazis?"

"No," said O'Mara, "I don't. I mean the Nazis who employed him *here*. Lelley's employers were in this country."

"I see . . ." said Therese. "I see . . . Shaun, it's like a novel."

"Truth is a damn sight stranger than fiction," said O'Mara tritely. "Anyhow, Ricky Kerr, who had a good record, was put in to deal with Lelley. He dealt with him. There was a car accident arranged at Nelswood, and Lelley was killed and that was that. But they knew all about that. They knew on the night that Ricky Kerr went down to Nelswood what he was going to do. They knew this was their chance to pick Ricky up after the job had been done and get next to *our* organisation. That was what they wanted. That was what they were prepared to sacrifice Lelley for. Well . . . they did it. The night that Ricky went down to Nelswood somebody was on to him. Somebody was wise. And that somebody was at a party at Glynda Milton's where Ricky was before he went down to Nelswood, and able to tip the wink to our friends that Ricky was on the job."

Therese said quickly: "My God . . . ! At Glynda's party. You mean . . . you mean . . ."

"I mean Miguales," said O'Mara. "That was the boyo who did the dirty work."

There was a silence. Then Therese said softly: "Shaun . . . this is terrible . . . Miguales . . . who would have thought that he . . ."

"You'd be surprised at the technique of these boyos," said O'Mara with a grin. "They're awfully clever, you know, Therese. Well . . . when Ricky got back to London they had a tail on him. They followed him. They saw where he went, who he made contact with. And luck was with them. Ricky, as part of his job, was given a list of our agents in France—people who carry their lives in their hands *all* the time; people who get one hell of a deal from the Germans if they're caught—you can imagine, can't you? Well . . . that damned fool has to get tight. He goes into some pub and drinks a little too much, and they'd put in a very charming young woman just on the off-chance of something happening like that. Ricky fell for it. He went off with her and they got the list off him. Nice work!" said O'Mara.

"And you've no idea who the girl was?" asked Therese. "You've no idea at all? Can't you possibly find out—somehow?"

"I'm going to find out all right," said O'Mara. "Because Miguales is going to tell me." He sat up on the settee, put his arms behind Therese's shoulders, drew her back against his legs, kissed the top of her head.

"I've got something on Miguales," said O'Mara. "You see, sweet, they put a fellow in to keep observation on Ricky's flat. We knew about that. I got on to that gentleman and I dealt with him. In his pocket I found a note from Miguales. Apparently, Miguales had been having some sort of a row with this fellow. They'd fallen out about something—such people sometimes do. Usually it's money, and it would probably be money in this case—because Miguales is a Spaniard and wouldn't be doing that sort of work because he liked it, as a Nazi would do. He was doing it because he was paid for it. My belief is that he was getting scared and wanted to get out and they wouldn't pay him until he'd done his job."

Therese asked: "And you arrested the man who was watching Ricky's flat?"

"That man was found dead in an empty house," said O'Mara. "He'd been shot good and plenty. And we found the letter from Miguales on him. All right. My story is going to be that Miguales killed him. Well . . . his diplomatic passport isn't going to help him a lot there, is it? He can still stand a trial for murder."

Therese said slowly: "I see . . . but what good will that do, Shaun? You still won't know what you want to know."

O'Mara said: "I think I've been a little clever about that, honey. You see, Miguales is planning to leave for Spain to-morrow morning. He'll be leaving his flat about eight o'clock. Well . . . at seven-thirty . . . on my way round here to pick you up . . . I'm going to call on him. I'm going to call on him at the psychological moment when he's getting ready to leave. At the moment when he thinks he's safe. At the moment when he thinks he's been fearfully clever and done us all in the eye, I'm going to present him with a proposition."

She looked up at him with a smile. There was admiration in her eyes.

"You mean you're going to make him *talk*," she said.

O'Mara nodded. "And *how*," he said with a grin. "I'm going to give him his choice. Either he can stay here and face arrest and a murder charge that will finish him in any event, or he can come across with what I want to know. He can tell me who the mysterious woman was who picked up Ricky Kerr. He can tell me all sorts of things I've wanted to know for some time. If he likes to play, then he can go to Spain. If he doesn't . . ." O'Mara shrugged his shoulders.

Therese was silent for a moment. Then: "Shaun . . . you're fearfully clever," she said. "You really are. But supposing he's afraid of these people. Supposing he won't talk. He might be too scared."

He shook his head. "He'll talk," he said. "Miguales is white-livered anyway. Besides, he knows goddam well that if he gives that girl away we'll get what we want. Of the two evils he'll choose the lesser because he's that sort of man. He'll talk."

She said seriously: "You know, darling, I'm worried about you. One of these days somebody like Miguales is going to get angry with you and something might happen—something not nice. Still, for your sake I hope everything is like you want it. I hope he talks."

"It's all good, clean fun," said O'Mara. "And he'll talk all right. Then all I have to do is to telephone the information through to my friends and they'll look after it. And"—he leaned over and kissed her on the mouth—"then I'll come along here just after eight, and pick you up and we'll make tracks for Eire. And how do you like that, my sweet?"

She said: "I love it, Shaun. You're a clever devil. Sometimes I get a little frightened of you. You—"

The clock on the mantelpiece struck three—interrupted her. Therese got up quickly. She said: "Shaun . . . go away from here, otherwise when you do pick me up in the morning I shall look like the wrath of God. Instead of which I want to look *rather* attractive. So will you please go after you've had one more drink?"

O'Mara got up. He said: "Well . . . that's fair enough. Just one more drink."

She got it for him. O'Mara held up the glass. "Here's to you and to me, sweet," he said. "And no heeltaps." He drank the whisky at a gulp. "I'm on my way," he said.

She went with him into the hall, helped him with his coat.

"Be punctual," she said. "I shall be waiting for you, Shaun. And be careful. I'm beginning to be afraid for you."

She put her face up to be kissed.

After a while O'Mara said: "You should worry, my dear. I was born to be hanged. And don't keep me waiting. I shall be here at eight-fifteen."

He went out, closing the front door of the flat softly behind him. She stood in the hallway, listening to his footsteps as he walked down the corridor.

IV

The small alarm clock that stood on the bedside table beside O'Mara's bed began to tinkle. Its small, silvery chimes continued until he awoke and, sleepily stretching out a hand, switched it off.

He lay for a few minutes, yawning, rubbing his heavy eyes with his fingers. Then he got up, sat on the edge of the bed. He stretched out his hand for his cigar-case, selected and lit one of his small cigars; sat, contentedly smoking.

Five minutes passed. The clock told O'Mara that it was ten minutes to seven. He got up, put the cigar in an ashtray, went into the bathroom. He came into the sitting-room ten minutes later, shaved and dressed.

He felt tired, vaguely uncomfortable. Always towards the end of an assignment O'Mara suffered a little from nerves, worried about the *denouement* that was close at hand.

He moved to the sideboard, poured out a little glass of brandy, drank it. He wished he had time to make coffee; wondered if he had; concluded that he had not. He went to the telephone, dialled a number, waited.

Quayle's voice came over the line.

O'Mara said: "You know, Peter, you're an extraordinary bloke. You seem to spend your life sitting on the end of a telephone line. Do you ever go to bed?"

"I'm in bed now," said Quayle. "But I haven't been getting a lot of sleep lately. Do you expect me to sleep when I'm wondering and worrying all the time about you and your doings?"

O'Mara said: "You leave me and my doings alone. Between you and me and the doorpost I'm not doing so badly. However, to be serious, d'you think you could arouse our friend Ricky Kerr and get him to go along and see that Valoz woman. I think he ought to. And I think he ought to bring her in—*if he can*!"

Quayle said: "I wonder what you mean by that? Anyhow, I'll get through to him and tell him."

"He'd better get a ripple on," said O'Mara. "He'll need a car. Let him go round there and collect the lady and hand her over to whoever you decide shall receive her. It's just after seven now and I'd like him to be there by soon after half-past. So he hasn't got a lot of time. When he's done that he might come straight round to St. Ervin's Court, Miguales' place, in St. John's Wood. Tell him to meet me outside just before eight. And tell him not to be later because I shall be leaving there about that time and I don't intend to wait."

"All right," said Quayle. "Busy little bee, aren't you?"

"Somebody has to do the work," said O'Mara. "One of these fine days I'm going to be given a job that lets me sleep when I want and drink when I want with whom I want. One of these fine days. . . ."

Quayle interrupted: "One of these fine days you'll get everything you want. In the meantime if you're very good I might send you to Rio, some time."

O'Mara said: "That's all I go on living for." He hung up.

He re-lit his cigar, began to walk about the sitting-room, his hands behind his back. He came to the conclusion that he was suffering from stage fright; began to plan in case there was a slip-up, in case somebody did not run true to form.

That was the devil with some people, thought O'Mara. You could study them, come to conclusions about them, work out exactly what they would do in any given set of circumstances, and then, if you were unlucky, they promptly did something else. O'Mara concluded that if somebody did something else on this occasion it wouldn't be quite so good for quite a few people.

There would be too many explanations required; too much talking. Still, perhaps, once again, he could rely on his luck.

He realised that if he'd wanted to he could have made the coffee. He helped himself to another small glass of brandy, concluded that it was bad to drink brandy at just after seven in the morning; had some more. He felt better and the morning seemed less cold.

He put on his hat and overcoat, went downstairs, walked round to the garage where his car was kept. He drove, not too quickly, towards St. John's Wood.

It was twenty to eight when he arrived. He parked his car in a side street, walked quickly and quietly round to the side entrance of St. Ervin's Court. He glanced up and down the corridor. He saw no one. He walked along the passage that led to the front hall, noticed with satisfaction that there was no porter on duty, walked up the stairs.

Outside the door of Miguales' flat, O'Mara stopped, took some keys from his pocket. He began trying them, one by one, on the lock. Whilst he was engaged in this process he was thinking that it would be damned funny if, when he got inside, he found the place empty and the bird flown. That, thought O'Mara, would not be so good.

He found the right key, opened the door, went inside. The place was warm as if no windows had been opened and there was a smell of stale tobacco smoke that hung on the air.

O'Mara stood in the hall, listening. He could hear nothing. He crossed the hall, opened the door into the sitting-room, poked his head round. The place was in darkness, the black-out curtains still drawn. O'Mara fumbled for the electric light switch, found it, switched on the light.

He stepped into the room, stopped, stood leaning against the doorpost. He was smiling and if it was not a smile of happiness it was at least a smile of satisfaction.

Miguales' body was slumped over the small bureau in the corner of the room. He had been stabbed through the neck.

The bureau was covered with blood, which had trickled down the side of the desk and formed a dark pool on the carpet. In the right hand of the dead man a pen was still clutched in a spasmodic grip.

O'Mara stood quite still, regarding the scene with the practised, almost disinterested, eye of a man who has seen death in most of its violent forms and who is not surprised at the grotesque.

But Miguales had been surprised. O'Mara visualised the scene. Miguales sitting at the desk, writing the note which he had been asked, or ordered to write, and then, while he was doing it, the sudden blow, struck by a sure hand which had adequately put paid to the not-too-efficient operations of the late *Señor*.

O'Mara walked across the room, stood behind the dead Miguales, taking care to keep his feet away from the dark stain. There was a piece of paper on the desk, near Miguales' right hand which clutched the pen so fiercely. Written on it was one word . . . "*Received*" . . .

O'Mara grinned. That was very funny, that one. So Miguales had been taking the pay-off. Miguales had been paid some more money and was about to write the receipt for it when he had been stabbed through the neck. A fitting occupation for his last few seconds of this life.

O'Mara sighed and turned away, switched off the light, closed the sitting-room door. He went out of the flat. He descended the stairs quietly, went out by the side entrance. He walked round the back of the block. Fifty yards from the main entrance a car was parked. Ricky Kerr was sitting at the wheel.

O'Mara said: "Good-morning, Ricky. How are you?" He grinned. "And how's that nice wife of yours?" he said. "One of these fine days I look forward to meeting her."

Kerr returned a grin. He said: "I expect you will—fairly soon, I hope, O'Mara. Can I do something for you?"

O'Mara said: "Yes. Did you find that Valoz woman?"

Kerr nodded. "I found her," he said. "She was dead."

O'Mara said: "No? What do you think she'd died of?"

Kerr said: "I know. She took poison."

O'Mara said: "I wonder. Well, that's that. Do you think it looks like a good suicide?"

Kerr said: "It looked like suicide to me."

"Did anyone see you go in or come out?" asked O'Mara.

Kerr shook his head. "No," he said. "Nobody did. And there was no one in the apartment except the Valoz piece. I wonder why she decided to kill herself?"

"She didn't," said O'Mara. "Someone else did that for her. But it's just as well it looks like a suicide. Right . . . thank you very much, Ricky. That's all I wanted to know."

Kerr raised his eyebrows. He said: "Well, I am surprised. I thought maybe there was a little work in the offing. I thought maybe—" He jerked his head in the direction of the entrance to St. Ervin's Court.

O'Mara said: "No. There isn't any more work—well, not much." He smiled a little. "Someone has decided to liquidate our friend Miguales," he went on. "I've just had a look at him. He's as dead a man as ever I've seen, which I think is a very good thing."

Kerr said: "It looks as if something's been happening lately— or someone has been making things happen."

O'Mara said mysteriously: "I think so too. Well, so long, Ricky. I'll be seeing you some time." He went away.

He walked quietly round to the side street where his car was parked. He looked at his watch. It was three minutes to eight. He got into the car, started the engine. He drove rapidly towards Therese's flat. He wanted not to be late.

CHAPTER FOUR
A Farewell for Lovers

ALMOST as soon as O'Mara touched the bell-push the door was opened. Therese stood inside the hallway smiling at him.

She wore a small black and white check coat and skirt beneath a snow leopard coat, and a black turban. She made a delightful picture.

She said: "I was beginning to think you were going to be late, Shaun. You can't imagine my sigh of relief when I heard the door bell."

He said: "You don't mean to tell me you were waiting in the hall for me? Is it as bad as that?"

She said: "Do you know, I think it's as bad as *that*."

O'Mara said: "You damned liar!" He looked at her. His eyes were like hard diamonds.

He thought: How pitiful it is, how redundant and wasted that this woman, who looks so beautiful, who has such attraction, such ability to charm, should be so foul within. For her the arts of the harlot, the cunning of the monkey, the viperish tactics of the snake; that she who might have had so much to give should take so much from a world already stricken of beauty and peace.

Therese stiffened. Her voice became hard. She said:

"What do you mean? What is this?"

O'Mara said: "You wouldn't know, would you?" He closed the door behind him with a bang. He went on: "Go into your sitting-room, my sweet, and don't try anything funny. It's all over bar the shouting."

She turned on her heel, went into the sitting-room. Inside she faced him. She said:

"Shaun, I don't know what's happened—"

He interrupted: "Don't be a fool, my dear ... don't be a fool, Therese. You're much too clever to talk like that. And you've had a busy night, haven't you?"

She began to say something. He put up his hand. He said: "What's the good of talking? *You* know and *I* know we've done enough talking." He smiled at her—a sardonic smile.

Therese stood in the centre of the room, her arms hanging straight by her side. She seemed quite relaxed except that she was breathing a little quickly.

O'Mara said: "The trouble with you beautiful and clever Nazi babies is that you're so damned clever you never think of the little things."

She said: "No? So we clever Nazis don't think of the little things! Perhaps you'll tell me what I forgot. It would be kind of you, you—" The obscene word came easily to her lips.

O'Mara said: "Aren't you a beastly little thing? Knowing words like that, my sweet. So you want me to tell you what you forgot. I've been dealing with your sort of people for a long time. You always do the most stupid things, because your minds are so tortuous they work things out to such a degree that a thing that's obvious is seldom seen." He said: "Do you know, Therese, you might have got away with this except for that letter thing—the letter that Miguales wrote to you."

She raised her eyebrows. She said: "To me?"

O'Mara said: 'To you. Miguales wrote that letter to you and it began '*Dear Señora.*' You erased the 'a' so that it read '*Dear Señor*—' Then you planted it in the inside pocket of that white-faced rat that you sent to keep observation on Kerr's flat. You knew damned well that we were going to catch up with him, and you imagined that that would put us on to Miguales. You thought we'd do the same thing with Miguales as we did with your other employee. I refer to the late lamented Mr. Lelley. You thought we'd kill Miguales, which, of course, was what you wanted. Then you could have continued with your job here. You thought that with Lelley and Miguales out of the way we should have been satisfied that we'd cleaned up the whole gang. You thought that we might consider that the unfortunate Miss Valoz wasn't worth worrying about.

"Well"—O'Mara shrugged his shoulders—"I made you do the job for me, didn't I?" He laughed. "My God, Therese, you must have had a busy night," he said. "You fell for that line I told you—you fell for that little fable about my calling on Miguales this morning and confronting him with a proposition. You see, I did that before I came here last night. I knew where that woman was before I came here. But you believed that I was going to see Miguales this morning. You had to take desperate measures.

"When I left here you went round to the Valoz woman and dealt with her. Perhaps she was a good Nazi—perhaps she *did* poison herself. Perhaps you poisoned her. I don't care. Then you went along and had a show-down with Miguales. You killed Miguales, and there was just the chance that you were going to get away with it."

O'Mara took out his cigar case, selected a cigar, lit it. He said: "But I doubt if even you would have had the nerve to do these things if I hadn't arranged our little trip to Eire. You thought there was still a chance of making a getaway, Therese, didn't you? How marvellous it would have been if I'd come to the conclusion that Miguales had been killed by someone else; if I hadn't known you were responsible for it. Well, I might have come back here, picked you up, caught the plane, gone to Eire. I might have—*if* there'd been a plane; *if* the journey had been really planned. You might still have got away with it."

He sighed. "Heaven only knows what you'd have done to me in Eire. You'd have probably been on a good wicket. You've got so many friends there."

Therese said harshly: "All this is lies!"

"Rubbish!" said O'Mara. "It's all truth—all of it. And you know it. Do you mean to tell me that Miguales did *not* write that letter to you?"

She said: "Does it matter what I say? Supposing I said that he did not write that letter to me. Supposing I said that I'd never seen it."

O'Mara said: "You poor damned fool—your fingerprints were all over that letter."

Therese said nothing. She looked at him through half-closed eyes.

O'Mara said: "It's the old story. I've no doubt that some five years ago a Miss Therese Martyr did go to Biarritz—the place where you were supposed to meet Miguales. But I'll bet all the money I've got that she never came back. I expect that when we check up we shall find that the Miss Therese Martyr who went to Biarritz had no relatives in this country. Then you played the old game, didn't you? She disappeared in Biarritz and you came back as Miss Therese Martyr and you've been here ever since doing your job for the Fuehrer. Well, it's all over. All that remains now"—O'Mara smiled at her—"is the trip to Eire. My car's outside. Come along, Therese."

She said: "I don't feel at all well." She looked at him. "Do you think I might go to my room for a moment? I think you owe me that, don't you, Shaun?"

He said: "Yes, you can go to your room." He put his hand inside the breast of his jacket, brought out the Luger pistol. "But you wouldn't try anything else, would you?—not that there's anything to try. The game's finished."

She said: "The game is never finished. I may be finished—and my friends, but more of us will come. The game will go on—always."

She went through the opposite door into her bedroom She closed the door behind her.

O'Mara stood in the sitting-room, inhaling the pungent smoke from his cigar. Three or four minutes passed. He crossed the room, slowly opened the door of the bedroom.

Therese lay on the floor, huddled against the side of the bed. Her hands were pressed to her stomach; her face was ashen; her lips stained. As O'Mara came into the room she turned her eyes to him with a last conscious effort. Something green and terrible flittered in them as she looked at him. Then her head drooped; her body twitched spasmodically; her limbs relaxed. She was dead.

O'Mara stood looking at what had been Therese. He drew easily and contentedly on his cigar. Through his mind there flashed a series of pictures—the scenes in which Therese had starred.

A damned clever piece, thought O'Mara. A born intriguer—a born mistress of men—a born killer.

And this was the end of her conquests and her victories.

O'Mara shrugged his shoulders. Then he turned away, closed the bedroom door quietly behind him; went out of the flat.

O'Mara opened his front door; went into the sitting-room; threw his hat and coat on a chair. In the kitchen the woman who came in and did the flat each day was busy making coffee. She made good coffee. O'Mara could smell it.

He called out: "Good-morning, Mrs. Sykes. I'll have my coffee in here. Lots of it."

She went to the telephone, dialled Quayle's number. When Quayle answered O'Mara said:

"You can go to sleep now, Peter. Everything's on the ice."

Quayle said: "A clean sweep, Shaun?"

"A clean sweep," said O'Mara. "Therese did it all for me. Incidentally, somebody had better go round to her place and discover what's happened. She's in the bedroom. Sandra Kerr would be a good person to do that. It would be in the picture—don't you think?"

"You were always so artistic, Shaun," said Quayle. "Anyhow, I'll look after *that* part. And our Spanish friend?"

O'Mara said: "It was too bad about him—and Esmeralda too. I'm afraid Therese got very angry with them both. You can imagine what she could be like when she was *really* annoyed. Kerr can tell you all about Valoz."

"He's here now," said Quayle. "You take a rest, Shaun. We'll sweep up all the pieces."

"Thanks a lot," said O'Mara. "Oh, by the way, Peter, can I go off some time?"

"You're going off next week," said Quayle. "Believe it or not, you're going to Rio de Janeiro. It would seem that some of our not-so-nice friends are working much too much stuff over there. Our people there think that you might be useful. How's that?"

O'Mara grinned delightedly. He said: "Is this really true, Peter? Am I really going to Rio?"

"That's right," said Quayle. "You'd better come and have lunch with me. I'll tell you all about it. Well . . . so long, Shaun. Till lunch time."

O'Mara said good-bye; hung up. His eyes were sparkling.

Mrs. Sykes came in with the coffee. O'Mara poured out a cup; began to drink it. He put the cup down; went to the radiogram; put on a record—a *rhumba*. He stood, listening to the music, swaying his shoulders in time to it.

He left the record playing; went to the telephone. He asked for foreign telegrams.

He said: "This is Mr. Shaun O'Mara—Knightsbridge 66540. Here is a foreign telegram. You can send it deferred if you like—so long as it gets there in three days. Here it is—and take it carefully please—it's *very* important":

He said slowly: "The cable is to *Senhorita Eulalia Guimaraes*. The address is *25 Edificio Ultramar, Copacabana, Rio de Janeiro*. The cable is as follows:

"'*Tenho recordações maravelhosas Stop Adorote e sou sempre teu Stop até a vista Stop*.'

"The signature is *Shaun*."

O'Mara sighed. He said to the girl on the telephone:

"You be a good girl, my dear, and keep your fingers crossed, and one of these fine days somebody will send *you* a cable like that. I *hope*."

He hung up; went back to his coffee.

THE END

Lightning Source UK Ltd.
Milton Keynes UK
UKHW012001030322
399530UK00001B/149